chaletgirls

Slippery Slopes

EMILY FRANKLIN

NAL Jam
Published by New American Library, a division of
Penguin Group (USA) Inc., 375 Hudson Street,
New York, New York 10014, USA
Penguin Group (Canada), 90 Eglinton Avenue East, Suite 700, Toronto,
Ontario M4P 2Y3, Canada (a division of Pearson Penguin Canada Inc.)
Penguin Books Ltd., 80 Strand, London WC2R 0RL, England
Penguin Ireland, 25 St. Stephen's Green, Dublin 2,
Ireland (a division of Penguin Books Ltd.)
Penguin Group (Australia), 250 Camberwell Road, Camberwell, Victoria 3124,
Australia (a division of Pearson Australia Group Pty. Ltd.)
Penguin Books India Pvt. Ltd., 11 Community Centre, Panchsheel Park,
New Delhi – 110 017, India
Penguin Group (NZ), 67 Apollo Drive, Rosedale, North Shore 0632,
New Zealand (a division of Pearson New Zealand Ltd.)
Penguin Books (South Africa) (Pty.) Ltd., 24 Sturdee Avenue,
Rosebank, Johannesburg 2196, South Africa

Penguin Books Ltd., Registered Offices:
80 Strand, London WC2R 0RL, England

First published by NAL Jam, an imprint of New American Library,
a division of Penguin Group (USA) Inc.

First Printing, December 2007
1 3 5 7 9 10 8 6 4 2

LIBRARY OF CONGRESS CATALOGING-IN-PUBLICATION DATA
Franklin, Emily.
Slippery slopes: chalet girls / Emily Franklin.
p. cm.
Summary: Working at an exclusive ski resort, Melissa and Dove plan the Winter Wonderland Ball and try to patch up their love lives, while Harley is off in the islands with Dove's surfer boyfriend, and Dove is not at all sure what they are doing.
ISBN: 978-0-451-22231-2
[1. Resorts—Fiction. 2. Dating (Social customs)—Fiction. 3. Skis and skiing—Fiction. 4. Secrets—Fiction. 5. Caribbean Area—Fiction.] I. Title.
PZ7.F8583S1 2007
[Fic]—dc22 2007022314

Set in Granjon • Designed by Elke Sigal
Printed in the United States of America

For Kelsey and Tate

Slippery Slopes

1

"What are you going to do?" Melissa asks Dove as they walk toward the meet-and-greet party in the main house. Melissa keeps her voice low but can't hide the intense curiosity. She waits for Dove's response and surveys the scene around her.

The resort of Les Trois Alpes shimmers with the glow of the holidays that will unfold this week. Private jets land on the strip, each one filled with people expecting the very best from their mountain retreats. The famous and their hangers-on arrive by helicopter and chauffeured car, while the staff at Les Trois Alpes tries to anticipate the guests' every wish, stocking the suites with Egyptian high-thread-count sheets, fresh flowers, luxury chocolates, and vintage wines.

While their own dramas are about to unfold, Dove and Melissa know that the holiday week ahead is crucial in terms of tips and connections, the pressure turned on full blast for the Chalet Girls and their seemingly endless work. Holiday festivity is the theme all around them: Christmas lights twinkle from the large pine trees, illuminating the cold night air. Wreaths adorn the doors of each chalet they pass, and gentle music streams from the Main House. *It would be magical,* Melissa thinks, *if only I had someone to share it with. If that someone hadn't bolted at the first sign of conflict.*

"I don't know." Dove's voice is filled with doubt. "What am I supposed to do about this whole mess? It's crazy—I feel like my world could change in a matter of minutes." She thinks about her longtime boyfriend, William, far from the Alps all the way in the West Indies on the small island of Nevis. "Will's so great. Such a charmer. I really miss him. He's light and sunny and . . ." She stops herself from gushing. *Why do I feel as though I have to sell everyone on how amazing Will is? First I tried with my parents and they didn't get it. And with friends, I have to relay all the info about him. I guess that's the way it is with long-distance things. You don't have the luxury of showing off love in person. Or enjoying it yourself on a daily basis.*

"But then there's Max," Melissa reminds Dove, staring at her friend's cool reserve. At home in Melbourne, Australia, Melissa would never have been friends with someone like Dove—someone so poised and posh. *Even though Dove spent all of last week scrubbing toilets and mopping mud-caked floors, she still managed to be alluring. Meanwhile I managed to burn toast, fry meat when it should have been braised, and generally need guidance in all things cooking related. But at least I learned a few kitchen tricks. . . . Not to mention one or two non-food-related . . .* Melissa wonders if this week will be as demanding as the last. On the one hand, she isn't quite as green and knows how to stock the pantry. But on the other hand, Holiday Week comes with rumors of major expectations and big requirements—like the woman last year who wanted a champagne bath poured for her each night, and the guy who insisted on never eating the same food twice.

"Never mind the boys—how are we even going to deal with the rest of life here?" Melissa sticks out her tongue.

"Boys *are* the rest of life," Dove jokes, her smile bright in the dark. "We can always figure out how to shine on the job or at least fake it. . . . But you can't fake love."

"So, then, who's it gonna be? Surfer William or Moody Max?"

Dove swallows, her stomach churning at hearing both names aloud in the same sentence. “Right. Max.” Max who first stole her heart back at school in London. Max who still made her stomach flip, with his intense stare and amazing mouth, the way they could talk about everything from literature to Luscious Lava, his band. “If I don’t give him an answer by the end of the night, he’s leaving.”

Who’s it gonna be? I should have asked myself that question. Melissa bites her top lip as she and Dove approach the Main House. Dove has a difficult decision to make—but Melissa feels like she herself has no decision left at all. Through the window she can see them: both of them. Both guys, Gabe Schroeder and James Marks-Benton—aka JMB. After a big mix-up with them last week, neither one is speaking to her now. “I feel so stupid,” Melissa says. “How come there are a million cookbooks to teach even the worst chef, and not one good volume on love?” *That’s what I need,* Melissa confirms in her mind, *an instructional guide for love and lust. One that could rewind time so I wouldn’t be left with the mess from Turnaround Day.*

“I thought you were through with the ski-bum boys,” Dove says. Earlier in the day, Melissa had washed her hands clean of crushes, love, sex, and anything remotely related to Gabe and James. Even though, as Olympic hopefuls, they hardly qualify as ski bums. “You said—

and I quote—'I am swearing off all creatures male until I learn how to deal with them.' "

"Maybe I need to learn to deal with myself." *After all, I'm the one who liked two guys and got neither of them as a result. If only it were simple and the answer were as clear as James or Gabe, simple five- and four-letter names.* Tugging on her dark curls, Melissa smoothes out her black pants and looks at her outfit, hoping she's not underdressed for the pre-holiday week welcome. She sighs, half-full of nerves and half-filled with jitters. "I can't believe we're about to start this infamous week."

"Holiday Week." Dove shakes her head. "Capital *H.* Capital *W.* I remember coming here as a guest, back when . . ." She pauses. She doesn't add *back when I had money,* but that's what she thinks. *Back when I charged whatever I liked in the overpriced boutiques; back when my parents owned me; back when I hadn't left school, thrown away the opportunity to go to Oxford University, and gone out on my own.* She shakes off those memories and says to Melissa, "It was madness. . . . I'd do whatever I liked. Never thought twice about stealing bottles of champagne, sneaking onto the ski lifts at night. . . ." Dove gets a far-off look and then returns to the present. Those days of her trust fund and well-to-do parents harping over her every move are long gone. After her parents cut her off, Dove's job at Les Trois is mandatory. "Now I'm the one who'll have to clean up from the party."

Melissa looks back at the party and licks her lips, feeling the sting of cold air on her mouth. "What do you think Harley's doing right this second?" Melissa pictures their former fellow Chalet Girl, who left suddenly for the tropical island of Nevis, supposedly acting as a host there.

Dove narrows her eyes. "Probably on a plane, if I had to guess."

Melissa checks her watch. "She could be there already. Just think—she'll be in a bikini with a tropical drink in her hand while we're in wool sweaters, pining for guys we can't have." *Make that guys* I *can't have,* Melissa thinks. *How would I describe Gabe if I had to? Golden Boy on skis. And James? Coffee-colored hair, broad shoulders, and a laugh so contagious nothing could stop it. With my luck, neither of them will talk to me for the rest of my time here. And why? All because guys are stupid and competitive. Or maybe because I liked them both, never did anything about it, and now neither of them like me.*

Dove shivers, both from the cold and from knowing that Harley—beautiful, slightly dangerous Harley—will be on the same island with William. She doesn't want to give into paranoia, but it's hard not to let her mind wander. "What if they meet? I mean, how bizarre would that be?" Dove tries to fight an image of Harley in a string bikini, sidling up to William in one of the indoor-outdoor bars in the tropics. "You don't think she'd . . ."

Melissa grabs Dove's shoulder. "No. Harley's wild, but she's not mean. She'd never cross that line." Melissa delivers this opinion to Dove without any doubts, but once she's said it, she wonders. Harley left slightly pissed off about not getting any of the big tip money she and Dove got and annoyed that Dove had a choice of two guys, but mainly slammed by the fact that James—Harley's main reason for coming to Les Trois Alpes—hadn't been swept off his feet by her. Instead of going for Harley's long-legged outdoorsy glamour, James had been drawn to Melissa's easygoing nature, her sweet smile, her self-deprecating wit. "If anything, Harley's got a bone to pick with me, not you. Then again, she did win big by scoring a free trip to Nevis and a cushy lifestyle there."

Dove rifles her fingers through her new pixie cut, still shocked by how light her head feels after chopping off the foot of silvery blond she'd had forever. Her old best friend, Claire, from school in London, had the opposite hair—darkest black and shiny. Together, they'd looked like fairy-tale girls. Dove looks at Melissa, glad to have a friend like her rather than one like Claire, who lied to try and get Max, abruptly ending any friendship back home.

"If I don't say it enough—or at all—thanks for being here," Dove says. Melissa gives her a grin. "We should go in. It's time." She points to the Main House, where staff and guests mingle, where decisions have to be made. "Oh, man." She tries to suck in a full breath. "Do I tell Max to stay?" She bites her lip. "Asking him to be here is like breaking up with William." She looks torn.

"Look," Melissa says, balling her hands into fists as she spies Gabe and James with a cluster of ski-bunny girls around them. "Let's just take a deep breath and dive in—we sure as hell can't do anything from out here."

2

"So, now what?" Melissa turns to Dove once they're inside the Main House. Carols and holiday music fill the air, mixing with international chatter and clinking glasses. Boughs of spruce line the enormous fireplace mantel, giving a deep scent to the air that mixes with other seasonal smells from the food.

From a buffet table Melissa takes a cup of mulled wine and sips at it so she looks busy. *I won't stare at Gabe and James,* she thinks, determined not to give in to her crushes, the mix-up of emotions. *I won't let myself be one of those people who can't let things go. Just because I had something with gorgeous Gabe and still have feelings for James, I can't let them know. What was it Harley used to say? If you let guys know too much, it gives them all the power.* Melissa sneaks one look, hoping James will be checking her out, but he's not. Instead, he and Gabe are still in a swarm of other Chalet Girls. Melissa looks away.

Dove searches the room, scarcely noticing the over-the-top holiday décor, due to distraction on the romance front. "Where is he? I mean, if I have all of five minutes to give Max my decision, he better show up." She scans the table for something to eat. After choosing a frosted tree-shaped cookie and eating it, she says, "Mel, when you're cooking this week, make something like these. But not in the shape of trees."

"Too cliché?"

"Exactly." Dove can feel her heart slamming faster as she checks the crowded room for Max. *He'd stand out in the crowd—so tall, he's always able to find me anywhere. He was the one who'd walked across the grand ballroom at his parent's estate to dance with me, the one who found me at Les Trois.* And yet she'd given up so much for William—gone against her parents' wishes, lost her trust fund, seriously swerved her future away from Oxford University to stay here with him. *And yet he's not here*. Dove shakes her head. *Which way to go? What else will I have to give up?*

"Have you made your decision, then?" Melissa asks.

Dove does a deliberately slow nod, considering

each time her chin goes down. "My grandmother always used to say—in her very upper-crust Queen's English—that you've met the right person when they cross a room for you."

Melissa makes a dubious face. "That doesn't seem so big."

"No, listen. Imagine being in a fairy tale or something. One of those massive ballrooms. And in the sea of people, making eye contact with someone far on the other side." Dove does this now, finally locking her gaze to the corner of the room near the tall Christmas tree, and seeing him. Max, in his rumpled white button-down, his hair over his forehead. "If the person is the best match, my grandma meant, he'll go through anything to get to you." Max meets Dove's stare. Dove squeezes Melissa's hand. "So, yeah, I've made my decision." *I'll have to cancel my trip to Nevis to see William, and basically break up with him, and all for a possible something with Max. . . . But it could be worth it, right?* Dove tries to calm her pounding chest by eating a sugar-crusted cookie.

Melissa thinks about Dove's change of heart, wondering if James would cross a room, climb a mountain, or even deign to speak to her. *Maybe I have no match.* Laughter erupts from where Gabe and James are entertaining the bevy of girls. *I won't get jealous,* Melissa thinks but feels her gut twisting, anyway. *I don't care if they get together with someone else. It's not like I ever got to be a couple.* Then she reaches for a cookie, knowing that being a couple is exactly what she wants, what she wanted all along since she saw James (then known as JMB) on her first day. How his smile totally set her at ease, how the rest of him made her swirl with excitement. She stares at a green pillar candle and bites the inside of her lip, thinking, *Though, if you want to get technical, it's Gabe I liked first—a lifetime ago, way back in my faint memories of last season.* "Are you going or what?"

"Okay—as soon as I catch my breath," Dove says while she chews the last of her cookie. "I'm going to tell him." She looks again through the crowd for Max, expecting to find his eyes on hers, but this time, he's not there.

Melissa scans the table for something else to eat, wondering what foods she'll make this week. A wave of relief floods through her when she remembers she's not so new at her job. Not that she's an expert, but that at least she knows how to work the ancient stove in the chalet. She watches Dove swig some wine, feeling bad that her friend is still stuck cleaning toilets and making the guest beds. "Did I ever tell you how well you handled the crappy cleaning job?"

Dove shrugs. "No. But I'll accept the compliment now. Okay. I'm ready." *I'm going to tell him. Make my choice, and stick with it. Max. Here. With me.* A smile plays on Dove's mouth as she flashes forward to spilling her feelings to Max and having him sweep her up—literally and figuratively—in his arms. Dove licks her finger free of green frosting, savoring the sweetness, and then—all of a sudden—having any trace of sugar instantly sucked out of her. "Oh no." She clutches Melissa's forearm harder than she ever has.

Concerned, Melissa's eyes grow wide. "What? Dove, what's wrong?"

All Dove can do is stand there, her hands shaking. "There." She points subtly with her elbow so Melissa will look.

Standing with her hands on her hips, in front of the tree, is a girl so poised and beautiful, so shockingly stunning, Melissa blurts out, "God—she looks like an angel."

Dove makes a noise like she's just been slapped. "No. Not angelic. In fact, far from it." She lets a small gasp escape her mouth. "I can't believe this."

"You *know* her?" Melissa checks out the dark-haired beauty again, this time noticing that many eyes in the room are doing the same thing. She swallows hard when she sees that Gabe is clearly entranced. "Okay—who the hell is she?"

Dove crosses her arms over her chest. "That piece of work is Claire. Or, for those requiring a bit more information, Lady Claire L'arance Beale Strong. LCBS."

"BS . . ." Melissa grins.

"Exactly. She was my friend. My best friend. And I never thought she was mean—or that she'd . . ." Dove stops, suddenly aware that not only is it odd that Claire is at Les Trois, but that she's here, in the room. She stands on tiptoe, trying to find Max, searching for his dark hair above the clusters of people.

"And now she's not, I'm guessing?"

Dove ducks so that Claire won't see her. "Claire lied to get Max away from me—she ruined everything. I wouldn't even be in this mess if it weren't for . . ." Dove abruptly ends her sentence. "I have to go. I have to find Max before more trouble starts."

Melissa tries to calm her down. "Maybe Claire's come to say she's sorry?"

Dove's pixie face looks hard and sure. "Not a chance. She told me herself—what Claire wants, she gets." The fun kind of heart pounding Dove had switches to panic, and she bites the inside of her cheek, ducking behind people to get to Max so she can tell him about her decision. So she can get to him before Claire does.

After an unsuccessful attempt at infiltrating the group of girls waiting to talk to Gabe and James, Melissa decides she's had enough of the meet-and-greet cocktails and heads for the door. *Besides,* she thinks, *I have a long day ahead of me tomorrow. Shopping, cooking, preparing the menu for the week. Maybe I should try to make duck. Dove said it's not as complicated as it seems and it would be a . . .*

"Ah, just the person I was looking for."

Melissa lets her thoughts of cooking go as she stands face-to-face with Matron, the head of all the Chalet Girls, who looks like a stereotypical librarian with her long skirt and practical brown cardigan, her hair in a bun. "Melissa Forsythe." Matron looks at the clipboard in her hand and crosses something off. "How have you enjoyed your time at Les Trois thus far?"

For a second, Melissa wonders if she's about to get canned. *Have I done anything wrong? Um, maybe fraternized with the guests, but I haven't committed major faux pas, right?* "Yes. Yes, I have." Melissa plasters a bigger-than-normal smile on her face to show just how enthusiastic she is. "Really. I love it here!" Just as she says this, she notices James and a couple of ski girls heading toward the mistletoe in an arched doorway. *Did he just look at me?*

"I'm glad to hear it." Matron looks at Melissa, waiting for something.

Shifting her feet, nervous, and also distracted by the mistletoe, Melissa adds, "In fact, I was just going over this week's menu in my head."

Matron's mouth twists into a frown. "Well, that won't be necessary. . . ."

Crap—I am *being fired. Now what? Back to Australia? Back to reality?* She glances at James, who for certain is not glancing back, and wonders if being sent away would be for the best. Then she could leave her heartache behind once and for all. *No—maybe running away isn't the solution. Maybe going after what—or who—you want is.* "Please . . . I need to—"

Matron raises her eyebrows and checks her list again. "Melissa Forsythe. Your job as cook has been terminated."

Melissa's hand flies to her mouth in protest. "But I—"

"No *but*s, please. Instead, you will be the host for this week." Matron tucks her pencil into the metal clip on her board and continues. "With Harley, ah, away so suddenly, I needed to fill the spot. As a result, I've moved you up." She gives Melissa a firm look. "You'll need to pull far more weight than she did. Entertain your guests. Show them the sights. Ski with them. Regale them with stories."

Regale them? Ski with them? Melissa's head swims with too much info at one time. Not to mention the fact that the ski boys are officially under the mistletoe, the other Chalet Girls and leggy, long-haired lustfuls moving in on James and Gabe like flies to syrup. "I'm the . . . host?" Melissa says the job title disbelievingly. "I'm taking Harley's place?"

"Yes." Matron clears her throat. "Why the sad face? I thought you'd be happy with the promotion."

Melissa nods. *Then who will cover my old job? At least*

I'm not fired. And I could make more money. But now—so long to the job I just figured out, and hello to new stresses and socializing. "So I have to plan the events?"

"You'll have to help plan, of course." Matron smiles, ever the tour guide. "Let's see—the Luxury Scavenger Hunt, Ice Painting, and of course, the most important, the Winter Wonderland Ball. I'm sure you'll pass with flying colors. Just remember—holiday week is our most precious time at Les Trois."

Melissa nods, the full realization of everything hitting her hard. *People come here for a glamorous end to the year, dumping piles of money into their holidays. And what do we do? Serve them. Humor them. Tend to them. Some holiday for us.* She reaches for the door, knowing she wants to clear her head in the cool air, enjoy one last night alone before a week of nonstop parties and conversations. *Harley might not have been the most attentive host, but she was fun and smooth. I wonder if she's just as laid-back on Nevis. What if I'm terrible? What if I . . .* Then she scratches her head, tugging at her dark curls out of habit. "Matron? If I'm host, who'll cook?"

Matron consults her trusty list. "Lily de Rothschild."

Dove. Well, at least she won't be stuck with a mop and bleach. And she's already accomplished in the kitchen. Melissa looks over her shoulder to see if she can find Dove and tell her the big news. Instead of finding her, she sees Gabe directly under the mistletoe. He looks up at the sprig, then right at Melissa and winks. *He winked at me? Am I supposed to rush over there? Kiss him? Scream?* But Melissa doesn't have time to decide on any action before Gabe is in lip-lock with one of the nameless leggy girls. James looks like he's next in line. *So much for meet-and-greet. How about sex-and-next?* "I have to go." Melissa's voice is shaky. "I'll be sure to welcome all the guests first thing tomorrow morning." Fighting tears, Melissa nods at Matron, and bolts out the door.

Dear Mel and Dove-

By the time you read this I will be way tan and way relaxed—at least, that's the hope!

So far, life away from the chalet leaves me little to complain about: private plane here (thanks to my brilliant host family), free drinks (and a hostess who turns a blind eye), and my only responsibilities are taking care of the teen queens. . . .

We'll see what happens next!

Tropical love and kisses (from what I've seen, I want some of those!)—

HARLEY

3

Chills run their course from Dove's neck down her back all the way to her toes when she's finally close enough to Max to tell him. *How do I say it?* Stay with me. *Or no, that sounds like a command. How about* I made my decision. *Or* You're right, Max, there is something between us.

"Max." Dove says his name and breathes deeply. He leans one hand on the wall, towering over small Dove, and staring at her intently.

"Lily." He corrects himself right away. "Dove."

Tension fills the few feet of space that separate them. Dove wonders if she should leave words behind and just reach for him, but then figures he needs to know. "I made my decision."

Max takes a step closer to her. Close enough that she thinks she can smell wine on his breath. Close enough that she can see the spot on his face that he missed shaving. Close enough that if he wanted to, he could kiss her without much effort. "And?" His tongue traces the outline of his mouth and Dove wishes she weren't so nervous saying all this.

If only I didn't feel as though asking him to stay meant losing William forever. But that's what a choice is, I suppose, letting one thing go so you can reach for the next. She decides to just say it, simply and easily. "Max, I feel that you and I had . . ." She starts to say that they had something back in London but that what they could have now is even better. But before she can get it out, before Dove can reconnect with Max, someone beats her to the punch.

"You did *have* something—past tense being the crucial part of that statement." Claire smirks as she says this. Shaking her long, dark hair so that it swishes onto her back, she walks past Dove and stands right next to Max. "See? I told you, Max. She's just using you. Just like before."

"Claire—what right do you have to even . . ." Dove gets out only a few words before Claire tramples her.

"I'm a paying guest. Not like you these days." She

raises one dark eyebrow at Dove, her lips perfectly gleaming with gloss, her cheeks pink. "Same as Max."

Max sticks his hands in his pockets and looks first at Claire, then at Dove. "Look, Dove, just so you know . . ."

Dove looks at Claire's hand, how close it is to Max's, and wonders just how long Claire's been at Les Trois. How long she's planning on staying. If Max had invited her all along. "You don't have to explain. I understand completely." She points to Max, feeling her plans crushed. "I don't care what you two do—just leave me out of it." Tears sting her eyes, but Dove refuses to show the emotion. Instead, her voice is steady, reasonable, the same voice she used to tell her parents she didn't want their money, didn't need their support. "Stay, go, do whatever you want, Max." She starts to walk away.

"Don't you have anything to say to me?" Claire asks after Dove. "After all this time?"

"Claire, don't." Max's voice houses concern.

All three of them immediately flash back to Max's eighteenth birthday, the black-tie party, the night everything changed. Dove whips around. "No, Claire, I have nothing to say to you. In my mind, you don't exist." *Except she does,* Dove thinks. *She does and yet again she's ruined everything.*

The morning light brings a refreshed sense of power to Melissa.

"Just because I'm not supersuave doesn't mean I can't handle being a host, right?" She pulls her hair into a ponytail, slides into her black pants and red shirt, and does a last look in the mirror before heading upstairs to wait for the guests.

From her top bunk, Charlie groans. "It's too early for all this. I want a vacation. When Matron said I'd be replacing someone in The Tops, I thought for sure I'd be the host. Not your old maid position."

I'm not an old maid, Melissa thinks, wrinkling her brow. "Look at it this way," Melissa says. "Last week you dealt with crap from toddlers as the nanny; this week you'll only have to deal with real crap. . . ."

"That's disgusting." Charlie sits up and rubs her eyes. "While you guys were out having fun last night, I was here polishing the brass by the fireplace."

Melissa wrinkles her nose. "I wouldn't say we were having fun, exactly. . . ."

Charlie jumps out of bed, landing with a thud on the cold floor. "I thought everything was supposed to be festive this time of year. Stockings, menorahs, trees, lights."

"Festive, yes. Fun, no." Melissa recalls Gabe and his mouth-to-mouth, and the way James gave her nothing but silence. "It's not like we get to have a holiday of our own, you know."

"Holidays are what you make them." Charlie smiles, making her freckled cheeks wide. "Did I hear rumors of you and a certain ski guy?" Charlie runs her fingers through her tousled strawberry-blond hair and instantly looks put together. Melissa wishes she had those kinds of looks. Not movie-star gorgeous, just honestly lovely.

"What rumors were those?" Melissa blushes. "I'm not usually the kind of person who has rumors spread about them."

Charlie shrugs and slithers into straight-legged pants and a turtleneck. "Maybe you're not the kind of girl you think you are." She pulls her socks on. "I'd love to stand here and gossip all day but I have two mudrooms to clean and you—Miss Host—have to go entertain the masses. After all, people want their Christmas days jam-packed with fun and food."

Melissa nods. "Hey, I was so crazed last night I didn't even think to check the guest log. Who do we have the pleasure of hosting?"

Charlie's face shows a massive grin as she gestures with her broom. "Correction—*you* have the pleasure of hosting. Apparently, some didn't like their luxury hotel rooms and wanted to check out life in the chalets." Charlie bows as though the guests are entering the room.

Melissa starts out and then turns back. "But who are they? Aside from disgruntled ex-hotel guests?"

Charlie taps Melissa on the shoulders like she's a

fairy godmother and her broom is the wand. "That dubious honor goes to the ski team. That's why I was asking about any unsubstantiated rumors." She pauses and grabs the dustpan. "All those guys are staying here."

I won't freak out, I won't freak out, I won't trip over the bearskin rug and fall on my ass. I will not offer the guests champagne and spill it on myself. I will not humiliate myself like I usually do. Melissa surveys the large living room, knowing that though it's empty right now, in two minutes it will be filled with this week's guests. Her guests. Including one guy she kissed, Gabe, and the guy she wishes she did, James. *I won't mess up, even if I have to pretend I know what I'm doing.* She puts her face to the window, looking out at the path that leads to the chalet.

"Anyone there?" Dove calls from the kitchen.

"Not yet." Melissa checks that the doorbell works, and then goes to find Dove. "Could I be more nervous?"

"Yes, in that you could actively be fainting or vomiting." Dove slides a sheet of croissants into the oven and checks her watch. "Five minutes and the breakfast buffet will be served. I'm making a traditional Christmas pudding for later—it's de rigueur for Les Trois." She pauses, remembering holiday meals at the resort as a child. "They always serve it warm with brandy butter."

"Sounds incredible." Melissa shakes her head in awe.

"How'd you get all this done so fast?" She opens and closes the pantry doors, taking in all of the newly purchased goods, the organized way that Dove has prepared a gourmet spread. *It took me ages to find my way around the kitchen. Let's hope hosting comes more easily.* "Was that the doorbell?"

Dove rolls her eyes. "No, that's your imagination playing tricks on you."

"Well, it wasn't my imagination last night when Gabe and some girl were going at it under the mistletoe." Melissa reaches for a cranberry scone but then stops herself, knowing if she eats it now she'll just get crumbs everywhere and look less presentable.

"Are you jealous?" Dove spreads out layers of crumble cake onto sterling silver trays, readying the food for the guests, wishing that her own night had gone differently.

"I'm not jealous. It's not like I want Gabe. . . ." She shrugs and doesn't mention whom she does want. "Except we did have fun. There was this whole other side to him, like when he and I were on the mountaintop. . . . He was sweet, romantic."

Dove shakes her head and wipes her floury hands on her apron. "I'm beginning to think that guys just don't change. No mater what." She considers something. "Girls, too. Look at Claire. Evil then; same thing now. Only better hair."

Melissa winces. Bad enough to have unresolved feelings for someone—worse when they clearly like someone else. "I can't believe they're all going to be here." Melissa shows her hands to Dove so she can view their shaking.

Dove hands Melissa a double-sized bottle of champagne. "By *them* I'm guessing you mean him, right?" Dove gestures with her chin to the living room.

Melissa turns, gripping the champagne bottle as James unzips his coat, drops a heavy duffel on the ground, and looks right at her.

4

Dove rushes through the last of her lunch preparations so she can try and catch a shuttle van into town. Despite the holiday, the shopkeepers have open hours, never wanting to turn away the extra cash flow of splurging vacationers.

"I've had it," she says to Charlie. "I've decided my whole life right now is maybes." Charlie licks her pointer finger and slides it along the last tray she has to wash, scooping up scone crumbs, and waits for Dove to go on. "Sorry—I know we don't exactly know each other very well."

Charlie smiles. "I know enough to say good luck."

She takes one more fingerful of crumbs before sliding the tray into the soapy water. "And yum—if the crumbs are this good, I can only imagine what the actual pastries taste like." With no dishwasher, cleaning up from meals takes ages, but Charlie doesn't seem bothered. *In fact,* Dove thinks, *nothing seems to bother her. I wish I had that kind of calm personality.*

"Thanks. Next time I'll save you one." Dove unties her apron and attempts to hear what's being said in the dining room.

Charlie watches her. "Listening for anything in particular?"

Dove shakes her head. "No. Well, maybe. See? Here I am with *maybe* again." She helps Charlie by sponging off the counter, thinking about seeing Max last night, how thinking of him with Claire makes her physically ill, and how now that she never asked Max to stay, the thought of him leaving makes her feel sick, too. "What do you do when nothing in life makes sense?" Dove sighs. "Maybe I'll be with Max, maybe I'll be with William, maybe I'll stay here, maybe I'll go to Nevis. My brain cannot bear the indecision any longer." Dove clutches her head like she's in a migraine ad. *I wish I were on the beach right now. With William beside me and a fruity drink in my hand, with nothing to do but be with him. The countdown has begun.*

With her hands covered in soapsuds, Charlie gestures at Dove, sending blobs of slippery soap onto the floor. "Wait a second. Maybe you'll think I'm sounding oversimplified here, but what exactly do you want?"

These words make Dove stand still. *How do I explain it? What exactly do I want? And why is choosing so hard for me?* "You know what it is? I feel like every decision I make changes everything—all those tiny moments when you leave the house and miss the bus, or take this job or that . . ."

"Or like this guy or that . . ."

Dove smirks. "All of those add up. And what if I make the wrong choice?"

Charlie empties the sink of soapy water, adjusts the faucet to the right temperature, and then sticks her whole head underneath. A minute later she swings up, splattering Dove and the counters with her wet head. "So much better than the no-water-pressure shower downstairs." She takes a kitchen towel and pats her hair dry. "I don't think there's such a thing as the wrong choice. Look at me. I was living in L.A., going nowhere as a nanny to people whose job it is to fill the pages of the tabloids. I take a kid for a walk, blah blah blah, and now I'm here."

"Washing dishes and cleaning loos?"

Charlie swats Dove with the towel. "Fine. So maybe my job prospects haven't changed dramatically, but I've saved lots in tips, collected tons of contacts on every continent, every country, every state—and I figure when the time's right, I'll move on."

"So you take each day as it comes?"

Charlie twists her thick wet hair up into a messy bun and nods. "When it comes to life, my philosophy is, Whatever is meant to be will happen."

Dove thinks about Max's intense stare, the way his hands felt on her back the last time they'd kissed. Then she switches to sunny William, his laid-back attitude and gentle good looks that make her feel lighted from the inside. "And what about love?"

For the first time, Charlie's face responds without looking upbeat and unfazed. "What do you mean?"

"I mean," Dove says, wiping the counter again and trying not to slide on the wet floor, "if you're able to just relax about where your life's headed, what does that say about your approach to love?"

Charlie's blue eyes narrow and her freckled face pales slightly. "Love's different. I firmly believe that if there's something—someone—you want in this life, you have to seek them out." She pauses. From the dining room, they can hear Melissa's voice rising as she tells a story. Only certain words are audible—*snow, ski lift, fell down, mess*. A big eruption of laughter filters through, causing Charlie's eyes to light up.

Dove studies her. "What?"

Charlie blushes, the pink coming though her thickly

freckled skin. "Promise you won't say?" Dove agrees. "Did you hear that laugh, his laugh? That's what I mean." Charlie eyes the door, anxious to peer through it.

"Wait—now you're the one who isn't making sense." Dove checks her watch.

"I like someone." Charlie grins.

Dove waits for her to say more. *If I get into town soon, I can see about any price changes in the West Indies tickets. And if there's any way to leave before New Year's—maybe even sooner. What if I could get on a plane tomorrow and be with William? Maybe that's the trick to choices—just doing something before your mind takes over.*

Charlie takes a deep breath. "When I was nannying last week, I saw this guy at one of those clubs. One with a snow theme, or whatever."

"And?" Dove raises her eyebrows, making her whole small face look expectant. More laughter from the other room makes her smile. *Good for you, Melissa. Even though she must be so nervous with Gabe and James and all their skiing buddies in there, she's holding her own. For now.*

"And I've seen those movies, and read those books where a person feels they're destined to be with someone." Charlie undoes the messy knot of hair and her strawberry locks cascade in wet waves. "And that's how I feel about someone."

Dove's curiosity gets the better of her. "Okay, who is this man of great mystery?"

Charlie drags Dove by her collar over to the doorway. They open the swinging door just a crack and peer through. "Him," Charlie whispers. "James."

"She what?" Melissa stomps the snow off her boot and holds the door open for Dove. In town, the cafés are busy with people scarfing down lattes before their morning ski runs, the shops swarming with pre-holiday shoppers. Melissa has all of ten minutes before she has to head to Dolly's to shop for prizes for the Luxury Scavenger Hunt and masks for the Winter Wonderland Ball.

"She likes James. What can I say?" Dove pays for a small coffee, hesitant to part with even a few coins after trying so hard to save her money. The travel agency was jammed when she went in, and they'd asked her to look online if she wanted to change her travel dates.

Melissa sticks her tongue out and finishes her coffee in three big sips. "I like Charlie, I do. But she was there when Gabe and James and I . . ." Melissa remembers the scene unfolding during Changeover Day—Harley leaving for the islands, James finding out about Melissa and Gabe's hookup before Melissa could even explain that she'd liked James first. "So what is she planning on doing?"

Dove shrugs. "Don't know. I mean, from the sound of it, she's pretty determined to get your man."

Melissa kicks Dove under the small café table. "He's not my man."

"But you want him to be. . . ."

Melissa wipes her mouth on a small waxy paper napkin. "Listen, I'm shirking hosting as it is—I have to run. Between the scavenger hunt tonight and the ball coming up, I don't know what to get to first."

Dove counts on her fingers. "One, scavenger hunt is lame and no one goes. Don't waste your efforts. Two, the ball is a big deal and people want something original. Three, you come first, so don't forget to deal with what you want, too."

"And you?"

"I have to find a computer and see if I can get to William sooner than planned."

"I wish I had one to lend you, but . . ." Melissa thinks. "Any public terminals?"

Dove shakes her head, momentarily sidelined. Then she gets it. "I know—Matron. She has that massive wall of them in her office."

Melissa looks at Dove like she's gone crazy. "Um, yeah, in her private, off-limits office." She stands up, clears her cup and saucer, and warns Dove. "Don't let love send you packing. And by that I mean, Don't get busted. I need you here."

5

Dolly's Warehouse hulks into the white sky, the brick exterior set back from the street and filled to the brim with trinkets and treasures. Once inside, Melissa takes a form and miniature pencil, along with her budget notes, and begins searching for ideas for the ball. *If Dove says the scavenger hunt isn't a big deal, fine. We can just give coupons for prizes, or bags of candy—something small. But the Winter Wonderland Ball is something else.*

Pictures from balls past lined the walls of the Main House. Dating back to the 1920s, the balls had been major affairs, complete with horse-drawn carriages, exquisite dresses, and themes that rivaled Hollywood award shows. Three years ago the whole resort had been turned into Venice, Italy, with the snow colored blue to look like water and sleds made to look like gondolas. The year after that had been Snowflake, with a three-ring circus of events, each one more elaborate than the last. But last year's event is the one that Melissa can't shake off. *How can I compete with a murder mystery party that was so intricately planned that international papers were convinced the death was real and picked the story up, only to have it turned into a movie?* The girl who'd planned that was whisked off to Los Angeles to come up with other ideas for films.

"Can I help you?" a salesman with a mustache asks Melissa.

"Just looking," she says. "For the Winter Wonderland Ball," she adds, so he doesn't think she's browsing for no reason. As soon as she says that, his face changes.

"Ohh, planning the ball. Come this way."

From his pocket he produces an old-fashioned skeleton key and leads Melissa behind trays of jewelry, boxes overflowing with expensive perfumes, and gift bags filled with name-brand clothing and sporting gear.

"Where are we going?" Melissa asks, more than a little wary of following this salesman to God knows where all by herself. "No offense, but I have to get going on this project. And I'm meant to be at the chair lift in an hour." *Skiing with the professional ski team,* Melissa thinks, remembering breakfast and how it was all she could do not to crawl across the table and into James' lap, telling him everything. Instead, she took Matron's advice and regaled the team with stories to make them laugh—mainly at her own expense. The time she fell off the lift and wound up in someone's lap, the time her snow pants ripped on the way down and caused a big draft. They'd laughed at those tales, even James—though he refused to look at her. *It's like I repulse him,* Melissa thinks as she hesitantly follows the salesman through a creaky metal door. *If I were Charlie or Dove, I'm sure James wouldn't look away.* Gabe, meanwhile, had given her more than one lascivious look, as if to announce to the entire table that he'd kissed her, that he'd gotten to her first.

"Here we are. Backstage."

Melissa steps inside the cavernous room and gasps, the sound echoing over the amazing spread before her. "Whoa. Wow. Wow again."

"Feel free to look around—and when you decide on a theme, let me know."

To her left are life-sized elephants made out of papier-mâché. To her right, a full-sized merry-go-round. In front of her, animals of all shapes and sizes, giant tea cups, costumes ranging from queens and kings to devils and angels, as well as chandeliers and strings of multicolored beads illuminated by track lights.

Talk about inspiration. They have everything. Suddenly,

the photos in the Main House don't seem out of reach. All I have to do is come up with a kick-ass theme. But what? Melissa wanders the room, her hand resting on a jack-in-the-box as tall as a tree, then passing by a yellow-brick road all rolled up. *Wizard of Oz? Has it been done?* She pauses, her brow furrowed. *Surfing—no. Ice Age—no. Something without boundaries.* From outside, the bells chime, alerting Melissa to the ticking minutes.

"Sir?" She calls out to the salesman.

"Yes?"

"Can I come back? I just can't . . . I'm rushing and I'm worried I won't . . ."

"Fine with me," he says. "I'll even give you the key if you like." He stares at her, bemused. "Don't look so shocked—it's not unheard of. Plus, you have a nice manner. I bet you'll come up with something wonderful." He hands her the key.

Melissa slips it into her pocket, takes another look at the wondrous collection of objects. *Maybe something will magically occur to me if I close my eyes.* She tries it. *Nope.* "I'll be back," she says. *I don't know when I'll find the time, but since the ball is happening so soon, I'd better figure out a way.*

The back door to the Main House won't budge. Dove tries to pound it open with her knee, but she can't, and doesn't want to risk making a scene. Guests with skis jauntily perched on their shoulders and other staff members walk by, which makes Dove flinch. *If I get caught, I'm done. I won't even be able to afford to get to the airport for my flight to Nevis, let alone have fun once I'm there.*

"Hey, Dove!" Charlie shouts from the very end of the gondola lift line. "Coming up?"

Do I look like I'm heading for the mountain? Dove wonders, but smiles and just shouts, "Nah, not right now. You have fun!" Charlie waves, then goes back to inching forward in line. Dove uses her hand as a sun visor, checking out who else is in line. Sure enough, James is a few people ahead of Charlie. Dove watches her try to worm her way ahead in line so she'll be in his gondola. *She's so determined,* Dove thinks. *Melissa better act fast if she wants to get James' attention.*

Dove gives up on spying and on the back door, and instead traipses around the front. Inside the Main House, the stately room is nearly empty, with just one chalet worker on the pay phone, speaking in rapid French. Dove, who is fluent, understands what the guy is saying, that he misses the person on the other end of the line, that he wishes she could just come here.

"*That's it!*" Dove says aloud before clamping her mouth closed with her palm. *I can ask William to come here. He has funds put away from all the boat charters he's had. He can come here, be with me, and then we'll go off together after New Year's!* She goes to Matron's office and tentatively knocks on the door, even though she knows Matron is at her pre-Christmas planning session with all the cooks. Not only is Dove skipping out on this (*I'll blame it on being new,* she thinks, knowing this might not fly), but now she's breaking one of the cardinal rules. Thou shalt not enter Matron's office uninvited.

This would be so much simpler if I had my laptop and wifi, she thinks. But her parents stripped her of most of her belongings, feeling that since she was choosing to leave her Oxford University acceptance behind, she could do without the luxuries they'd bought for her—computer, designer clothing, jewelry, and, primarily, her large trust fund.

Dove takes one last look around to make sure no one's watching and then slides the red barrette she had clipping her bangs out of her hair. First she bends it all the way open, then, once it's shaped like a wide *V*, she carefully slides one end into the door's lock while simultaneously leaning on the door and turning the knob. All this she does with practiced silence, and despite a pounding heart and racing pulse, she manages to slip into the office without anyone seeing.

Hardly a sigh of relief passes before Dove perches in front of the computer, knowing that she has only five minutes before she runs further risk of anyone coming back from the meeting. Quickly, she wakes the computer from its sleep and tries to log on. Only after the security screen comes up does it hit her—*Of course, how stupid of me; Matron obviously has it locked.* All that risk of breaking in, for nothing. Dove thinks about stomping her foot on the ground out of anger but knows the threat of being heard is too much. She tries one more time, typing *Matron* as the password, but of course it's no good. The screen remains locked.

"Damn!" Dove whispers, and the moment the word escapes from her mouth, she hears the doorknob turning.

Even though Charlie manages to score a ride up the middle mountain with James, it's Melissa who succeeds in grabbing his attention.

"So, what do you think of chalet life so far?" Charlie doesn't look at James, feeling that most of the time guys like it when she seems distracted, like she has better things to do than talk to them.

Shoulder to shoulder with members of his ski team and other well-heeled guests, James shrugs. "I guess it's too soon to tell." He looks at Charlie, but she looks out the foggy glass window. Below, skiers and snowboarders swerve gracefully down the powdery trails, ant-small from the gondola's height.

Charlie accidentally-on-purpose stumbles, and

clutches James' arm for support. He helps her, and momentarily they have hand-to-hand contact. *If only he wasn't wearing gloves,* Charlie thinks. Her own hands are bare, specifically for this purpose. "Well, let me know if there's anything I can do to make your stay more comfortable."

James smiles, looking down at the mountain. A few days and the slopes will be jammed with spectators, camera crews, and journalists all vying for a shot of the Olympians and hopefuls as they compete for top place in the Trois L'or, the international race. Even though its name means "three golds," only one medal is given. And nine times out of ten, that gold medal means a similar feat at the winter games.

"Oh, no," Charlie says, shaking her lustrous hair out from her ski hat. "I forgot my gloves. How silly of me."

James looks at the sweet girl and does what any good person would. "Here," he says. "Take mine. They'll be huge on you, but . . ."

"Oh, no, I couldn't do that. Really, it's so nice of you, but . . ." Charlie plays coy—not annoyingly so but enough to seem even more endearing.

From the other side of the gondola, Melissa has the displeasure of hearing the entire exchange. She tries to get a view of James and Charlie, fighting the urge to wiggle through the crowded car. Bending down, she can see only Charlie's hair and James' arms. *He's giving her his gloves? That's so nice. But also, crap, she does like him. And clearly he's at least noticing her.* Melissa tries to chat with the other team members she's hosting, but it's tricky to make conversation while trying to eavesdrop.

"Thanks, James. You're so sweet."

Gag. Gag. Melissa rolls her eyes and then notices the gondola is nearing the mountaintop. *Fine—if he wants to be a knight in shining Gore-tex, that's his deal. I have people to entertain.*

"If you'll step this way," Melissa says, graceful for once as she exits the blue gondola, "we have a choice of double diamonds to the left, jumps to the right, or, if you're up for a challenge, the little-known secret path."

Using the word secret *always attracts attention, and this time's no different,* Melissa thinks as most of the skiers head her way. The guests with cashmere accessories and overly plump lips due to augmentation head for the small gourmet restaurant Sommet, "the summit," where small salads set diners back far too much cash for the staff to ever go. *Someday,* Melissa thinks, *I'll treat myself to a meal there. At night, with the stars. Probably by myself.* But she shrugs off any thoughts of a nonromantic future and focuses on the task ahead.

"I thought this trail was closed." Gabe Schroeder points to the small, snowy inlet with his pole.

Melissa tries to forget that she knows what Gabe's lips feel like, that she let herself be wooed by such a notorious womanizer. "No, not closed. Just restricted."

Fine, so maybe it was closed, but the cool factor I'll have if I can pull this off will more than make up for the fact that Charlie's wearing James' gloves and that the two of them are having what looks to be heavy flirting disguised as a snowball fight.

"Great," one of the teammates, Pierre Luchese, says, his accent making the great sound like he's coughing up phlegm. "We go down 'der and exploration."

"Exactly," Melissa says and starts off on her skis. "Exploration."

As the group begins to push themselves past the gondola station, they weave through snow-heavy pines and onto a narrow trail dotted with small jumps. "Cool path," Gabe says, sidling up to Melissa. Once others have passed them, he adds, "Hey, are you ever gonna get over things?" He says *things* as though he didn't lead her on, didn't know that James liked her, and that forgetting all the recent happenings would be as easy as drinking water.

Melissa stares at Gabe. *Sure, he's still hot, but knowing what's inside of him—sleaze—makes him less appealing.* "You know what, Gabe? I'm sure Les Trois has a dense female population."

"Meaning?" Gabe does a trick, spread-eagle over a jump, all the while still looking at her.

"Meaning," Melissa says, trying to navigate the trail but finding the deep powder more difficult than she thought, "surely there must be enough estrogen elsewhere that you don't need me to forgive you in order to have a fun holiday." And having gotten a decent word in, Melissa decides to leave Gabe to stew in his own good-looking slime. She pushes off with her left leg, catching up with Pierre and Gabriella Cordesi, the Italian Junior Pro, who leads the pack.

"Great idea, Melissa," Gabriella says. "I'm loving this trail."

"Thanks," Melissa says. In her mind she gives a nod to Harley, the one who first told her about the trail. *Now she's far from the snow, basking in the glow of the beach, bronzing without a care in the world.* Melissa wishes just for a second that she'd been offered the job on Nevis, if only so she could be away from James and Gabe, enjoying a change of boy scenery as well as climate. *James hasn't said two words to me or even looked my way. Guess whatever we had before has melted faster than the snow.*

Charlie giggles from a clump of pine trees where she's conveniently fallen—not a big misstep, just enough to require the aid of a certain someone. "Thanks, James. Here you are, coming to my rescue again."

"No problem," he says. His orange-and-black down jacket shows his broad shoulders, his cheeks are ruddy from the cold air. Paused on the slope, he sticks his hands in his pockets.

"You must be freezing," Charlie says. She gestures with one of his oversized gloves. "Here, take this back."

Before James can answer, and before Melissa hurls onto the mountain from listening to Charlie try to snare James, someone shouts. *Maybe he never really liked me at all,* Melissa thinks as she breathes hard into her jacket collar. *Maybe he would have always preferred Charlie.* "Hey, look over there—the rope!"

James turns. "I thought that was a Les Trois myth—the tale of the rope swing."

Gabe shoots back, "Nope, it's real. And I'm going for it."

Coiled around the trunk of an impossibly tall fir tree, the rope swing has clearly seen better days. Melissa explains it to the group as she skis over to it, intentionally not looking at James. *The truth is,* she thinks as she sees the orange of his jacket out of the corner of her eye, *it isn't just that I'm jealous of Charlie—or of anyone flirting with James. The truth is that I liked him so fast and so much, that letting go of all that is hard. But it'll be easier this way—easier to drop all interest in guys and focus on my job.*

Her breath comes out in white puffs, small clouds pluming into the air. *He made me laugh and just knowing I lost my chance with him makes me—*

"Hey, you, Melissa Forsythe," Gabe taunts. "Dare you to go first."

"I might be a lot of things," she says jokingly, "but stupid isn't one of them. You're mad if you think I'm testing that thing out." Melissa uses her pole to unwrap the heavy rope from the tree trunk, her pulse speeding at the thought of actually swinging on it.

James swishes over, with Charlie following closely behind. "No way I'm going on that," she says. She looks adorable in James' gloves, her form-fitting ski outfit, her hair bright against the navy blue of her parka.

Melissa looks at her roommate and at James. *They make a good couple, actually. She's perky and pretty, and he's everything.* She imagines snapping a photo of them and how they'd look like a couple in a catalogue. With a sinking feeling she realizes she'd never look as perfect as that.

Without warning, Gabe drops his poles, climbs backward to get some leverage, and then in one quick motion gives a yelp. "Whoo—check it ooooouuutt!" he yells as he grabs the rope swing, propels himself through the cold air, does a 360 in the air, and lands perfectly.

"You idiot!" James says, half kidding and half not. "Why risk wrecking your knee before the race?"

Gabe smiles, out of breath, excited from the buzz of jumping. "You gotta live, man. Can't hang on to every hope and dream."

He means it in a laid-back skier's way, but Melissa reads between the lines. *He's right. I mean, I can't cling to a vision of being with James forever. It'll only keep me from ever moving on. After all, I'm making new strides all the time. I didn't know how to cook, learned the basics, and was a chef last week. I'm semisocially incompetent, and here I am leading professional skiers down a secret trail.*

"I'm next!" Melissa shouts. She makes her way backward the way Gabe did, with the other skiers smiling at her. Only James gives her a look of disbelief.

"Mesilla . . ." he says before correcting himself. *Mesilla*'s been the name he thought was hers. Part of the reason for the whole confusion last week. He'd told Gabe he liked a girl named Mesilla; Gabe had written it off at first, but once Gabe learned it was the same Melissa he'd hooked up with, he hadn't told either James or Melissa. "Melissa, this might not be the best idea."

This stings Melissa like a sharp wind on her face. "Gabe tested it out," she says, throwing his name into the mix just out of a need to protect herself. "If he can do it, so can I."

James sends a pleading look to Charlie, who tries to stop her. "Melissa, maybe James is right. I mean, he and Gabe know a hell of a lot more about skiing than . . ."

Melissa's stomach turns over at the thought that Charlie is stepping up for James. *They're even acting like a couple, communicating with looks, those unspoken words that suggest a deep connection.* If anything, having Charlie doubt her only makes Melissa more determined. "It's no big thing. Back home, I surf killer waves in waters where shark attacks aren't uncommon. I think I can handle this." And without further exchanges or stopping to reconsider, Melissa drops her poles, flings herself forward with all her might, speeding right to the rope swing. *You can do this,* she thinks. *Just reach for the knot, hang on, and go for it. It's all about being strong and letting go of the past, reaching for the future, and . . .*

Melissa feels her hands grip the rope just like they're supposed to. With her thigh muscles tensed, her legs leave the ground, her skis wobbling in the air. *I'm doing it!* She grins wildly, laughing. *And I'm not even scared, even though I'm way up high.* She looks down at the spectators—Gabe clapping, Gabriella and her friend Camilla shouting things in Italian, Pierre looking bored, and Charlie with her . . . with her arms around James. In the split second that Melissa sees this, is witness to James returning the touch, her grip on the rope loosens just enough that right at the very peak of swinging out, Melissa feels herself falling out of control.

Dove and Melissa—

Don't know if you got my first postcard, but disregard everything in it. Life here isn't exactly what I pictured. Sure, there are beaches, but let's just say I've been put in the dog's quarters while the rest of the family is living large in the largest resort house you've ever seen. (Can you say five pools?)

But life isn't all bad . . . The social scene is mellow-cool, with beach bonfires, private soirees, and beautiful sandy boys just waiting to be SPFd. If I get a day (or, um, an hour) off, I know where I'm headed. . . .

Hope mountain life is decent—I do miss the slopes.

Yours in bikini land,

Harley

6

Dove's entire body feels as though it will explode with fear as the door to Matron's office swings open without a knock. *I'll just start crying,* she figures, *that might work. Pull the old having a breakdown, needed solace, and so forth.* Then she pictures Matron's stern face and knows that plan will never work.

"Look, I'm really sorry but I . . ." Dove brushes the wisps of hair that frame the sides of her face, biting her top lip as the door opens all the way.

But rather than Matron's puckered face, she is instead confronted by a completely drenched and rather annoyed-looking Max. In a blue half-zip striped sweatshirt and jeans, he stands dripping onto the carpet. As if it's not at all bizarre that he's sopping wet and in Matron's office with a startled Dove, Max wipes a rivulet off his nose and tilts his head to the side in greeting.

"Bit of a problem with a frozen pipe." Max's voice is normal, as though nothing's happened. "The problem being that it burst. On me."

On you alone or on you and Claire? Just thinking about Claire and her ravenlike sheen, her cruel smile, is enough to make Dove fume. "Sorry you're wet," she says, but rather than having it come out angry, she can't help but laugh. "You look ridiculous."

"Thanks." Max grins at her, his eyes cast downward, wanting to convey more emotion than just humor. He gestures wildly at Dove, intentionally flicking beads of water at her. "That—that is why I'm here. Reporting problems to Madam Matron, as it were." He raises his eyebrow and flicks again. "And what, may I ask, brings you here?" His forehead wrinkles. "How'd you get in?"

Dove swivels in Matron's desk chair, pretending she never even touched the computer. "I'm just leaving, actually. Tried to come in here for . . . just to . . ." The computer screen doesn't fade right away, though, so Max stares at the password and then at Dove.

"Ah, right. If memory serves, you no longer have a laptop."

Dove gives him a hard look. *That's not all I don't have. I might not have had William if I'd asked you to stay,* she thinks but doesn't utter. "No—poor little me. Without modern forms of communication."

"All the modern ones suck, anyway. People should go back to writing letters, and then we'd see where things really stood."

Dove shakes him off. "Meaning what?"

"Meaning . . ." Max clenches his hands, which are red and cold from the freezing water. He starts to shiver. He smiles at her but then the grin fades. "Who were you trying to e-mail?"

Defensive, Dove stands up, trying to leave the office and Max behind. "I'm late for cooking. I have to go." She can not only see but feel him shake, his sweatshirt sending tiny rivers of water down his wrists. Dove fights the instinct to hold him, to try and warm him up.

"Les Trois."

Dove stops. "What?" *Maybe the water has frozen his brain—obviously we're at Les Trois, but what does that have to do with anything?*

"The password." Max's eyes flash, but his voice remains steady. "I happened to be here when Matron threw a bit of a computer fit last week." Max's lips are ringed with blue, the shaking now infecting his whole body. "I don't know who you needed to get in touch with . . ." Max gives Dove a look that lets her know he's completely aware of what she was going to do online. "... But you must really have wanted to—you know—to break in here and all."

"I didn't break in." Dove feels a lump rising in her throat. *Am I upset about being caught? Or upset that Max knows about William?* "And just so you know, I wasn't e-mailing. I was just trying to change my ..."

Max shakes his head and holds up his palms like a traffic cop. "You don't have to explain." Dove feels frozen, knowing if she immediately types in the password she'll send a direct message to Max, but if she doesn't, she'll miss her chance to switch her plane ticket, to redirect the downward spiral holiday week has sent her way. "So?"

"So." Dove wishes she had the guts to make a move one way or the other. "You need a blanket. Or at the very least, a hot shower." For a second, she wonders if this sounds flirty rather than like concern for his well-being, then she decides he probably doesn't care. That Claire will be more than happy to lather him up if need be. From down in the village, the church bells sound into the winter air, sending noise that undulates around the buildings, up toward the mountains.

"I'm so late." Dove looks at the clock behind Max's head. "So, so late."

"Me, too," Max says, his voice softer and slightly shaky.

"For what?" Dove flashes to any number of things

Max could be late for: shopping with Claire as she gives her parent's charge card a beating, ice skating with her on the large pond, or perhaps writing about her in his thick leather journal.

"For this." Max puts his cold hands on the back of Dove's neck, where both the chill and the touch send her reeling. He's about to kiss her; in fact, he's leaning down, in a pre-kiss position and she isn't stopping him, when Matron appears.

Furious, her voice is shrill. "What in heaven's name is happening here? You've ruined the rugs—it's worse than snow damage." She furrows her brow at Max. "And you, Miss de Rothschild, aren't you meant to be in the middle of a proper lunch?"

Dove hasn't heard her last name used in a long time. She glances at Max, who is paralyzed from the interrupted kiss, his dropping body temperature, and from Matron's demanding presence. "I'm on my way now. Of course I made paninis in advance—roasted pepper with three cheeses, prosciutto and fig. . . ." Dove rattles on about the food while disappearing out the door.

Only after she gets outside and starts to run toward the chalet does she realize she, too, is shaking. Shaking, and with neither a changed plane ticket nor a kiss to show for it.

* * *

The quiet in the room is interrupted only by a steady-paced but quiet beeping. *Am I dreaming?* Startled, Melissa bolts upright, thinking that the beeping sound is her alarm clock informing her it's time yet again to be a host for the masses. But when she sits up and checks out her surroundings, the first thing that hits her is the stinging pain in her side.

"Ah . . ." She doubles over, clutching her rib cage.

"You broke two of 'em," Gabe Schroeder says. Late-afternoon sunlight streams from the window, casting a glow onto his silvery blond hair.

Melissa looks around. White curtains, white walls, white linoleum floors—like a version of heaven, except that Gabe Schroeder is sitting next to her. Once she sees the white jacket flapping toward her, she gets it. "The Infirmary? What the—" Then she remembers the dare, the rope swing, trying to look cool while Charlie got too close for comfort to James.

A doctor wearing an expensive striped tie, pressed khakis, and a French blue button-down walks toward the cot where Melissa lies. Covering her, though she is dressed, is a white sheet. *At least Gabe didn't see me naked. At least I'm not in one of those awful tie-in-the-back robes.*

"Miss Forsythe." The doctor gives her a standard look of concern crossed with a hopeful smile. "You had quite a tumble." Melissa blushes, thinking of the rope, how it slipped from her hands. His accent is thick, and Melissa strains to understand him. "You'll be fine." He hands her some over-the-counter pain medication and a tiny cup of water and warns her to be careful on the slopes.

The doctor gives her the go-ahead to leave. As he walks away, Melissa looks at Gabe and thinks, *I should be just as careful off the slopes.*

"Diagnosis: two broken ribs and one very bruised ego." Gabe's hand grips the metal bars on the side of her bed. "Not to mention an unrequited crush."

And just what am I supposed to say to that? "Speak for yourself—my ego's just fine, thanks." Melissa feels herself blush but ignores it. Gathering her strength she tries to move, and semisucceeds. "And what would you know about my love life, anyway?"

Gabe shakes his head. "Nothing. Nothing at all." He leans forward, looking closely at Melissa's face. "Just—I didn't think it was coincidence that you let go of that rope right when the hottie nanny grabbed James."

Melissa's throat tightens, her breath quickening. "First of all, Charlie's not a nanny. She's a cleaner now." Melissa wishes this small fact made her feel better, but the truth is that Charlie could be scrubbing toilets or making filet mignon or playing with rich toddlers, and the only part that Melissa would mind is the thought of James liking her. "And second of all, I dropped that rope because it was hard. Admittedly, it was a stupid trick." She leaves it at that. "Ow."

Gabe watches her touch the sore ribs. "The doctor said you could spend the night if you wanted."

"No way." Melissa sits up, then prepares to stand.

Gabe rises from the folding chair to give Melissa a hand. She refuses. "The doctor said spend the night. Or maybe he said you sure put up a fight—I don't know. The guy's Bavarian, so it was hard to understand. . . ."

This prompts a grin from Melissa. She steadies herself on the edge of the bed, swings her legs over the side, and stands up, wobbly. *Oh my god, pain. Pain. And also—more pain.* She blushes again, knowing Gabe's right and her ego is way bruised. "Fine. My ego might be dented, but at least I gave it a shot."

Gabe reaches for her again but accepts the shrug-off and hands her the comfort of her jacket. "Look, if it's any consolation, I think you were . . ."

"I don't need your consolations, okay?" She licks her dry lips and studies him. "What're you even doing here, anyway?" *Of course James didn't come, just Gabe.*

Now it's Gabe's turn to blush, which he does only slightly, then takes a deep breath. "Ski team code—if you see the injury, you accompany the injured. Done deal."

"And you stay with them? Me, I mean?" Melissa's side hurts, her whole body aches, and her mind begins to race with everything she needs to get done. "Oh, man. I'm doomed. How can I host when I'm among the wounded?"

"Okay. In answer to the first question—yes, I stayed. Not just because it's code. But because . . ." Gabe turns away from Melissa, looking out to the otherwise empty infirmary. "Because I'm sorry. As you know by now, I have this reputation—"

"Deserved," Melissa interrupts.

"Can I finish?" Gabe cracks his knuckles, biding time. "I acted like a jerk last week. Maybe that's too mild a word. Fill in with any insult you see fit. And I just wanted you to know that—I didn't mean to. I didn't . . ."

Melissa watches Gabe fumble, feeling both glad (*he deserves a fumble or two*) and sorry for him (*he looks like a kicked puppy*). "Why did you?" Wondering if this makes sense, she elaborates. "I mean, what happened between us, exactly? And why?"

Gabe covers his mouth with his hand, thinking, and then nods. "So—I'm kind of a self-admitted sleaze, you know?" A laugh escapes, but not funny, more pathetic. "And last year—when you liked me, I'd never really had that. Not the way you did. So when the team got transferred here, and boom, there you were . . . I just thought—Maybe it'd be a chance to—"

"Redeem yourself?"

"Something like that." Gabe waves the air with his arms. "Obviously, that failed. I don't know why I do it, really. When we were together . . ." His green eyes lock hers. "Don't for a second think I was pretending."

Melissa feels just the smallest amount of relief there. It's one thing to be wooed, but worse if you think the guy's lying. "So why do you do it, the womanizing thing? Being a player—roping innocent Australians into your dreadful schemes?" Melissa blushes again, thinking of how she fell for it—being with him on the mountaintop, naming stars and thinking they could be an actual couple. "I wish I hadn't been so naïve."

Gabe shakes his head. "No—don't say that. It's one of your good qualities." He holds open the door and Melissa wobbles out, trying to protect her bruised ribs and the rest of her body—heart included—as she navigates the hall.

Outside, in the parking lot that sits between the Main House and the Infirmary, Gabe waits for her. His boots scrape the pavement. "You sure you're okay?"

"Yeah." She feels it, too. Not only because the pain will ease up and somehow she'll deal with being the slowest host, the host who is unable to ski, but because when someone screws you over and admits to it, you're afforded a certain amount of relief. "Thanks for waiting with me." She pauses. "Even if you're still a bit of an ass."

Gabe grins. "I can't refute that." He starts to walk her toward the chalet. "You coming?" She shakes her head.

"I gotta go into town. Stuff to take care of. Think any

of the chalet guests will mind if I keep up my disappearing act?" She likes how *go into town* sounds mysterious, even though the job at hand is just planning for the ball.

"I'm happy to cover for you—say you're sleeping off the fall or whatever. You sure you're up for going anywhere?" His voice is doubtful.

She reassures him. "I'll be fine. Really. I can take care of myself, believe it or not."

"Oh, I believe it." Gabe slips something out of his back pocket, walks the few paces toward her, and hands it over. Their fingers touch in the exchange, both of them registering the small truce that has passed between them. "Before I forget—I have an invitation for you."

"Lucky me." Melissa smiles at him, accepts the envelope, and watches him walk up the path to the house before tearing open the sealed envelope. Addressed with just her name on the front, the invite is thick, cream colored, and set with dark green embossed writing:

Private Party

Please use this invite to gain access to:

A night of Chips and Dip

The site of the (c)old rectory, Isle Du Mont

NO RSVP REQUIRED*

**Admittance granted on the basis of secrecy*

What kind of party is this? I can't tell anyone about it? Melissa wonders as she makes her way to one of the Trois vans. *And where exactly is Isle Du Mont?* Isle *means "island"—why would there be an island here?* Melissa carefully slides the invite back into the envelope, wondering who else is invited, and since she's clearly not allowed to ask, what the code of silence means in terms of getting time off. *How can I disappear for a night with no good reason?* From her pocket she pulls the copy of a master key that works all of the vans, and opens the driver's-side door. First things first. *I'll deal with the Winter Wonderland Ball as fast as I can, then head back in time for dinner and some sort of hosting tonight.* As she turns the key in the ignition, Melissa wonders what's happening back at the chalet, if Dove is acting as chef and host, or if—and Melissa winces with this—Charlie has stepped into the role of showing the guests a good time. Like a good driver, Melissa adjusts her rearview mirror, checks that her seat belt is fastened, and though she notices it, doesn't pay much attention to the lumpy mass way in the backseat. *Someone's laundry bags? Sleeping bags? An orange jacket?* She shrugs—people were always leaving their belongings in the van—and heads, bruised, into town.

7

"You did what?" Dove shouts while trying to balance a tray with eight pints of Stella Artois on one hand while gripping a magnum of champagne in the other.

Charlie grins at her. Dressed in a black unitard that zips up the back, Charlie's outfit leaves little to the imagination. With cheeks flushed from the fireside heat, she leans over the bar and yells to Dove. "While you were off doing God knows what, I think I might have reached my goal." Charlie gives a meaningful glance up to the chalet's balcony, where James rests on his elbows, looking down at the growing party scene.

For Melissa's sake, I hope she doesn't mean what I

think she means, Dove thinks as she swerves in front of the bar with the tray. After leaving Matron's room, she'd come back to the chalet to find a party just beginning, with Charlie as the host. Now the soiree has grown to earthquake size, with Charlie at its epicenter, flitting this way and that trying to maintain some sense of order, while Dove slaves away making appetizers, whipping up dips of crème fraîche and chives, creating finger foods, and slinging the alcohol to calm the masses.

"What about you?" Charlie raises her eyebrows to Dove, relieving her of the champagne magnum as she's about to head upstairs toward James.

"What about me?" Dove asks, handing out the pints of beer and flashing back to Max, his hair slick with cold water, his hands shaking just like they did the first time he'd kissed her. "I'm just doing my job." *It's not that Charlie's evil or anything, just entirely focused on one goal: getting James. She's the kind of girl you can't ever really get to know, because the minute the object of her affection is around, she'll drop you.*

"Well, keep me posted on the gruesome details!" Charlie heads for the stairs, checking first to see if James is looking at her, which is unclear. He's still up in the balcony, but unlike in movies, when someone's far above you, it's not always easy to tell what they're looking at. "I'm off to try and interest a certain person in a tour of the guest rooms." She holds up the magnum like a trophy. "With this as the bait."

I doubt that's the only bait, Dove thinks, sizing up Charlie's body in her slinky catsuit. *At least she's still technically in uniform, at least color-wise.* She gestures to her with the last of the beers and then takes a drink herself, wiping the condensation on her slim-fitting black trousers. *I deserve it, after all,* Dove thinks. *Filling in for everyone while Melissa convalesces and Charlie social butterflies herself toward love, or at least . . . lust.* A look of concern washes over Dove's face when she thinks about Melissa and the fall, but from the way Charlie explained it, Melissa was being more than looked after. In fact, Charlie had been the one to encourage Gabe to ride along with the mountain patrol and stay with Melissa at the Infirmary.

"Hello," one of the guests slurs to Dove. In a tight orange T-shirt, Dove thinks the guy looks like a traffic cone, and she flinches when he tugs at one of the belt loops on her pants. "You're that bird girl."

"Excuse me?" Dove stifles a laugh. She doesn't want to offend the guy—after all, he's a guest—but his state of inebriation hardly gives him credibility.

"You know," Traffic Cone nods, his words mushing together. "The bird's name . . ."

"Oh yeah. I'm Dove." She points to herself, pulling on her cropped hair out of habit.

"You're the one she said used to have money or something, right?" He gives her a drunken leer and smiles. "Why would a good-looking girl like you go dropping a fortune behind?" He wobbles on one foot and for a second Dove thinks he might face plant into the carpet, which would suit her very well. *What an ass. Who brings up someone's personal finances? And more importantly, how does he know?*

"It's really none of your concern." Dove gives him her case-closed expression and sips again at the beer. *It could be worse; the Christmas carols could be playing on a continual loop, like they are in the rest of the buildings. If I hear "Joy to the World" one more time, I just might have to scream.*

"Aren't you supposed to pay for that?" A voice interrupts the party's hazy hum. Appearing behind Traffic Cone Guy is an even-less-welcome sight.

"Claire. I should have known." *I just might have to scream, anyway*. Dove feels out of place in her work uniform, and wishes she didn't care. *Sure, I'm off having adventures, following my own path and heart while Claire is stuck back at school in our old life, but still—it would be nice not to have any doubts. Particularly since Claire seems to have the ability to see right through any exterior I might have and into my core.*

Claire turns to the drunk Traffic Cone. "She's working here, you see. Really she oughtn't be consuming the beverages."

"Your friend's got a point." Traffic Cone nods.

She's not my friend. Not by a long shot. "Actually, as per the instructional guide handed out to all employees of Les Trois, section four, clause two states that, quote, 'While engaged in duties including but not limited to socializing, event chairing, and entertaining, or while off-hours, one may partake of the food and drink provided by the resort in a limited and mature fashion.' " Dove holds her beer in one hand, a bemused and steely eyed look on her face. "So you see, Claire, that not only am I allowed to be doing what I'm doing . . ." She takes a dramatic sip from the glass and licks the foam from her top lip while Claire and Traffic Cone stare. "I'm doing it in a mature way, which is more than I can say for you. Either of you."

Pleased with herself, Dove scrambles back to the kitchen to let out a sigh of relief. With her back to the party and her face toward the oven, she removes yet another tray of baked Brie and sighs. *I might not have reached William today, and I might not have changed my plane ticket to Nevis, but at long last I held my own with my nemesis. And that's something.*

"That was quite a rebuttal," Max says from the doorway. Long since dried off, he's the essence of rugged coziness in a red fleece and jeans. He's so tall he fills up the entire doorframe, and yet again catches Dove off guard.

As soon as she sees him, she tries to talk herself out

of her gut reaction. *He's incredible. If he marched in here and demanded I break up with William, what would I do? Agree.* With a large amount of blushing, Dove stares at the red fleece and the body in it and realizes she's already pictured herself wearing only that fleece. It would be long, like a dress on her, and she could curl up with Max, fireside, and—

"So, did you reach your"—Max stumbles over the word—"boyfriend?"

Dove returns to reality, where Max is getting it on with Claire, and William is a continent away, miles of ocean between them. *If I say no, I'll only appear weak and desperate. Why should I admit to being out of touch with William while Max has his own fling with Claws right in the living room?* "Yeah." Dove forces a smile. "Everything's cool." She searches Max's face for signs of disappointment but doesn't see any. "A week from now I'll be slathering on the SPF and . . ."

"Sounds like you have it all figured out." Max puts a hand on her shoulder and gives her a warm smile.

I guess he is fine with it. Fine with me leaving, going after William, with never finishing whatever we started. Dove knows she has to ask Max something but can't quite bring herself to do so. "What are your New Year's plans?"

Max removes his hand and shrugs, looking past Dove into the swell of partygoers. Dove fights the urge to follow his gaze. "Oh, you know, I'm not even sure how long I'm even staying here." He pauses and points to the ceiling. "As you're aware, I'm not staying right here, at The Tops, and being in the hotel isn't quite the same."

We can do this, Dove thinks. *We can be friends and chat about things like accommodations and holiday plans.* "I hear the hotel's really nice. That's what the ski team says, anyway." She laughs, determined to be breezy and friendly.

"It's fine. Five stars and all that." His face doesn't look like he's singing the praises of anything special, though. "But I miss it here." Max's eyes penetrate Dove's to the point where she has to look away.

Dove wipes her hands on a towel. "Suffice to say in terms of my cooking you aren't missing anything. And it's not as though Charlie's on anyone's Top Maids list."

"She doesn't seem like the dusting sort."

"Far from it. And Melissa—well, she's been rising to the title of host, but now who knows . . ." Dove thinks about Melissa, wondering if she should find her and bring her soup or something, but then she figures Melissa would want her to stay, to keep the party going as though she's here to host it. "So don't worry about what you're missing here. I'm sure the hotel has everything you need." Dove swallows as she looks at Max. *Why is life so complicated? Why does everything have to overlap—William and Max, jobs, holidays? If Max and I had stayed together I never would have met William. But if William hadn't taken the sailing job on Nevis I never would have had feelings for Max all over again. The two relationships are just inextricably linked.*

A whiff of Chanel perfume announces Claire's arrival before her words. Her bright red mouth forms a model-perfect smile. "The hotel really does have everything." She looks at Max and Dove as if it's all very normal, the three of them standing there. "They have fantastic room service. Don't they, Max?"

Dove feels a frown forming. "What do you want, Claire?"

Claire puts a hand on her hip, leaning toward Max. "The same thing as you, I suspect."

Dove shakes her off. "That's where you're wrong. I'm here working. A job? I know it's a foreign concept for you, but some of us need the money."

Claire raises an eyebrow and clears her throat. "We all need things, Lily." She shoots Max a meaningful look that raises a red flag inside Dove. *What exactly is going on with them? Are they together?* Dove wrinkles her forehead. *Why would Max tolerate Claire's rude behavior?* "Some of us need money or a job. And some of us just need to—"

Max claps his hands, startling Claire into silence. Then he speaks quickly. "We should go. Now. Dove, sorry to bolt but I think Claire here needs to get some rest."

Without putting up too much of a fight, Claire reluctantly nods. Then she squints at Dove. "Yes, I suppose I could use a good night. *In bed.*" She highlights the last two words and immediately grips Max's hand.

Dove stares at the two hands—Max's and Claire's—and thinks about finding them together at Max's birthday, and how shattered she'd been. *How could I have called Claire my best friend? She's so different now. Hard to believe she was the first person I used to discuss any problem with, my confidante in every way.* Max's fingers curl lightly around Claire's. Dove has instant recall for the way his fingers felt in her hair, the way his hand gripped her shoulder. *If I'm over him, really over him, why do I still feel some of that sting?* Putting on a brave face, Dove nods to them and goes off to manage the rest of the party. *For tonight, I'll be host for Melissa. Tomorrow, I'm heading back to the travel office.* The longer she stays, the more she'll have to confront those pent-up feelings for Max—and for Claire.

Chalet Girls—

Check out the front of this postcard! Is it the most fantastic view or what?! Lucky me, I'm experiencing it for real from my own new bedroom. Can't tell you exact details in a postcard (you never know who reads the mail these days), but let's just say the social life here is everything I dreamed of—and more.

Ran into (or, rather, surfed into) an old friend of yours, Dove, who was quite eager to talk. And Melissa, if you ever get tired of chasing ski bums around, head for the sand. It's warmer, cooler, and much, much more fun.

Yours with a tropical drink,

Harley

8

With the van parked in front of the supply store, Melissa slips the key out of her pocket and enters the large room. During the day, the place had seemed magical, filled with possibilities for the Winter Wonderland Ball, every inch devoted to amazing images. Now, though, with the night casting darkness through the windows, and shadows hulking in the corners, the place gives Melissa the creeps.

Two minutes, she thinks, making sure to leave the door cracked open. *No way am I going to get locked in here.* She lets out a small scream when she bumps into something solid, then laughs when she realizes it's a life-sized unicorn. The laugh makes her side hurt, which then makes her laugh more. *Okay, now I feel lame.* Still moving tenderly due to the overwhelming ache in her rib cage, Melissa slides her hand along the wall, hoping for a light switch, since the only other source of light comes from the main room, which only makes things more eerie.

Ah, success, Melissa thinks as her hand meets with a panel of switches. She flicks a couple of them only to find they do nothing. *Great—how am I supposed to find idea inspiration when I can't see anything?* Then she flicks the last switch. Strung overhead are what seem like millions of the tiniest blue lights; illuminated, the ceiling looks like a mountain sky at night. Seeing this gives Melissa a little shiver, and just enough light to make her way around the enormous room as she looks for the perfect theme for the party.

Icicles, fairies, Shakespearean dances—all too clichéd. Melissa rests her hand on one of the carousel's brass poles and looks at the odd collection of items around her: Greek columns, giant tribal masks painted green, yellows, and red, feathered birds, a shrunken castle, a mermaid with purple hair, and leaning everywhere, mirrors. Melissa thinks for a second and then moves so she can begin to sort through some of the stuff. She slides aside an oval mirror and then hefts a large rectangular one and puts them both near the merry-go-round. Reflected in them both, Melissa sees her own image. Her curly dark hair is slightly matted from lying down at the Infirmary, and she notices that she's leaning, cramped over just slightly to the left, no doubt from her injuries. In her pocket she feels the invitation to the secret party, and then she pulls out a pen and piece of paper, jotting down ideas, hoping that something will gel if she writes.

New Year's resolutions
snow
glitter

This is no good. Melissa shakes her head, annoyed. *I came all this way, with broken ribs, just to wander amidst the weird sculptures and mirrors. The last thing I need is to be confronted by a thousand images of myself.* She turns to avoid looking in the mirrors she's set up but finds even more mirrors to her left. She lifts the flap of a cardboard box and unearths even more mirrors, this time in the form of strands. Like Christmas lights, the mirrors are roped together, each one dangling a mini reflection, each one sending shimmers of blue light from the ceiling bulbs.

"That's it!" Melissa says into the empty air. *New Year, New You. Isn't that what we all want? To somehow wake up on the first of January with a new, better version of ourselves all ready to go?*

Working as fast as she can while trying not to bump anything into her side, she begins to amass all of the mirrors. There are wall-sized ones she can't move; smaller ones she can—each one unique. She can see it now—a hall of mirrors, elegant and magical, with candles and white lights, all done outside in the garden, sweeping down the path and culminating on the large frozen pond. Outside at night, Melissa knows the strings holding the mirrors won't be visible, and that the mirrors will look as though they are descending from the sky. Pleased with herself, she pauses for a moment by the carousel. In front of her is a rectangular mirror with etched sides. Angled upward, the looking glass shows her shoulders, but not her face, and also reflects the darkness behind her on the other side of the room. Melissa looks at the shadows via the mirror, wondering why the room seemed so scary at first. Then she sees something move. She peers closer into the mirror and sees it again—a shape on the other side of the room over by a ten-foot-tall fanged wolf.

With her heart thumping and her knees shaking, Melissa freezes. *Should I run? Scream?* Then she shakes her head. *No—it's probably a mouse. And while that's not the best thing, it isn't the worst.* She looks in the mirror but doesn't see anything else, and wonders if maybe her imagination is overactive. She checks her pocket to make sure the van key is there, and feels comfort at its hard edges. *Back to planning. By tomorrow, I'll not only be able to give an order for all of the stuff I need, but also for the food—kir royale, perfectly hued champagne drinks in tall flutes, whisked sugar sculptures that will look like crystallized breath. It'll be amazing. It'll be worth all the hassle of coming here, of—*

Melissa hears a noise and feels panic rising in her. *That couldn't be a mouse.* She turns around and squints into the darkness. *Yes, there's something there. Something? Or someone?*

Defying her fearfulness, Melissa tries to remember her old karate kicks as she propels herself into the darkness. She stomps her feet and then shouts. "I know there's something here. Just . . . show yourself." She bites her lip, her pulse blaring. "Don't hide." *Maybe this is foolish and I should be the one hiding.* Suddenly, this sounds like a great idea, and Melissa bolts over to the bear cave replica and ducks into its faux-fur inside. Crouching with her knees pressed to her aching ribs, Melissa is scared. *No one knows where I am—not Dove, not even Gabe, because I told him only that I was going into town.* Melissa tries meditation, breathing, and common sense to quell her fears, but nothing works, especially when she hears something. Not just a random something, but footsteps. Heavy ones.

Please don't find me. Please let me be invisible, she thinks as her entire body clenches with fear. Realizing the footsteps have stopped, she opens her eyes and nearly faints when she sees a pair of large black boots right near the entrance to the bear cave. *Please leave. Don't look over here. Leave.*

But it's no use. The boots walk toward her, causing alarms to ring in Melissa's head. "Stop right there. I know karate!" Melissa jumps out from the cave, figuring the best defense is battling the force of evil head-on.

"Well, then, call me surrendered." With his hands held up like he's about to be arrested, James looks baffled and amused.

Melissa's breath comes out in shaky gasps. She steadies herself on the rocky edge of the cave so she doesn't faint with relief, surprise, and left-over fear. "What the hell are you doing here?"

"Good to see you, too. I love greetings as warm as 'what the hell.' . . ."

A long silence grows between them. Melissa stares at the black boots, then her gaze travels up the length of James's body until she meets his eyes. The last time she saw him he was getting groped by Charlie. *Where is Charlie now? No doubt wondering where James is. Not that he meant to be with me or anything, but still.* "How'd you find me?"

"After I left The Tops, I fell asleep in the back of the van. So when I woke up, freezing, I might add, I stumbled around outside until I saw a light go on in here."

Melissa holds her hands in front of her now, the

fingers entwined as though she and James are holding hands. She remembers flicking the lights and points to the ceiling. "Blue. Kind of cool, huh?"

James steps toward her. "Very." He wanders around a little, with Melissa watching him as he eyes the merry-go-round, the battleships, the knights in armor, the papier-mâche hearts and snakes. "This place is incredible."

"I know. It's so great. All the potential . . ." She bites her lip, wishing hard that she didn't still feel the exact same way about James as she had the first day she met him. "Look at this." She shows James a snow globe that stands taller than both of them. The outside is clear; inside a plastic couple ice skates, their legs grounded to a plastic pond. "Anyway, there's just tons of stuff here." She doesn't want him to think she pointed out the snow-globe couple to highlight what they could have been, or that she's suggesting she still has feelings for him. To cover this, she motions to the giant wolf. "Now, that is worth getting creeped out about."

"Did I really freak you out?" James laughs and pats the giant wolf, calling to it as though it's a sweet, floppy puppy. "I'm sorry—I figured you knew I was in the van."

"Believe me, I didn't." Melissa thinks about the lump in the back of the van, how if she'd put two and two together she'd have realized the orange of James's jacket was the orange fabric she saw. "I thought you were someone's laundry."

"I've been called a lot of things in my life, but never laundry."

They laugh and wind up sitting atop two of the carousel horses, side by side. James has a large steed poised in bucking bronco position, while Melissa straddles a dappled grey, her legs kicking down to the stirrups.

"Guess we're not going to go anywhere," James says.

"I guess not." Melissa wonders if he means the horses or them. She holds her ribs while clutching the reins. "Can I ask you something?" James nods. "How come you haven't . . . inquired after my health?" She wants to ask him why he hasn't paid her any attention, not just about the accident, but can't bring herself to sound needy.

James coughs and swings his legs around so he's riding sidesaddle, and looks at Melissa. "Truth?"

Melissa's stomach rolls over. "Yeah."

"When I . . ." He starts but then stops. "I have this tendency to . . ." Shaking his head, he jumps off the horse and begins to pace in front of the carousel where the mirrors are lined up. Melissa watches James and the many reflections of him as he tries to explain. "You may or may not have noticed that I'm not the most forthcoming in terms of expressing myself." He doesn't wait for

Melissa to answer. "And the thing is that on Sunday, when the shit hit the fan and I found out about you and Gabe and . . ."

"Wait—I want to explain. . . ." Melissa knows now's her chance to set the record straight. That she semiliked Gabe, that it wasn't . . . how could she phrase it, though? Whatever way you wrote it up, it sounded like she never liked James that much. Or never liked him enough to do anything about it. *Words are one thing,* she thinks, *but actions are another.* Aren't actions supposed to scream while words whisper?

"You don't have to explain," James says. "I'm just saying, the reason I didn't ask about your fall—the reason I wasn't . . . that I didn't . . ."

Melissa jumps off the horse, wincing as she lands and the impact hurts her rib cage. With myriad reflections around her and tiny blue lights above her, Melissa takes an action that she hopes will scream as loudly as the truth. She wraps her arms around James's waist, looks up at him, and then, standing on her very tiptoes, kisses him.

Their lips meet in the slow motion way of films, with neither one pausing, just two mouths meeting for a small, gentle kiss. *This is it—I'm finally going to know what it's like to kiss him. To have his lips on mine. And he'll know how I feel. . . .*

But before James actually kisses her, he pulls back. "No—wait. We can't."

Melissa feels slapped. Foolish and rejected all at once. "Because of Charlie?" Melissa shakes her head. "You know, here I am thinking you can see past all the exterior stuff. Charlie's perfect legs and her amazing body . . . but you're just like everyone else, aren't you?"

James looks annoyed and dejected. "What? What does Charlie have to do with this?" He motions to her and to him. He waits for her to say something, but Melissa feels too embarrassed to say anything.

Never should have done that. What made me think I'm cool enough, suave enough, to risk that kiss? It's like the rope swing—I should stick to the paths I know and forget the rest. "You know what?" Melissa steps back. "Forget what I said. Never mind Charlie or falling on my ass or . . ." She pushes at the air as though she can move the comments away.

James gives her a weird look. "You sure you're okay?"

She nods. *I have to get us back on track. Like the beginning. If I can't be with him, at least let me be friends with him.* "Want to see the dinosaurs?"

"I can only imagine."

Melissa tugs the sleeve of James' coat and leads him to where small dinosaurs stand, mock-grazing. "Aren't they bizarre?"

"This one looks like he's about to slalom," James says, patting the side of a green raptor. "Except for the teeth."

Trying to belay the awkward air between them after the rejection, Melissa slings an arm around the neck of a brontosaurus and poses like she's in a photo. "Isn't this like a scene in a movie where we talk all night amidst all these strange and beautiful creatures?" She looks at James, thinking he qualifies as the latter. *We'll be friends. Friends would be good. We can hang out, I'll watch him race, he can watch me fall on my butt. . . .*

"It's exactly what you'd see in a movie. We'd exchange life stories and talk about what we did when we were kids and what we hope for in the future."

Melissa leans her cheek on the brontosaurus. "Should we?"

James smirks. "Maybe there's a fake palm tree or a bat cave somewhere around here." Across his face comes a look of true calm.

He's happy to be here with me, I think. Maybe friendship is the place to start—again. "We could look."

"Okay—first person to find the ideal place to sit and emote wins."

9

The entire resort of Les Trois is abuzz. With holiday music still piped over loudspeakers and wreaths on every available door, the buildup to tomorrow's Christmas celebration is bigger than the day itself.

"Come on! I don't want to be late." Hurrying along the iced paths, Melissa makes sure to stick to the salted and sanded sections so she doesn't trip.

Dove checks her watch. "You have eight full minutes before the race starts. I doubt you'll miss anything. . . ." Ahead of them, masses of people line the mountain's racecourse, with television crews, cameras, and reporters jammed in, all ruddy-cheeked and waiting for a winner. "Think they're nervous?"

Melissa rolls her eyes. "Just a tad. I mean, this race is the single biggest indicator of who goes on to win the gold medal at the . . ."

"Oh my god, listen to yourself. 'The single biggest indicator.' Hah. Who's been spending too much time with a certain pair of skiing boys?"

Melissa cuts across the back of the snowy expanse near the Main House. To the left she can see the holly-trimmed edge of the ice skating pond. In her mind she imagines the scene at night, when the ball is taking place, with everything silvery and perfect. *The world will glisten then, with decorations, music, and nothing will go wrong—except, of course, for the fact that I will be dateless for the evening.*

Dove can automatically tell what Melissa's thinking by the way her mouth twists into a frown. *It's the same expression I get when I think about Claire and Max.* "Mel—it's not like you'll be alone. . . ."

"But it's not the same thing. You have . . ."

"Max, I know." Dove's hand flies to her mouth and she cough-laughs in surprise. "Oh my god, I meant William. . . ."

"Sure you did." Dove and Melissa exchange a look. "Look, all I meant was that you're not really alone. You have—William." She says his name slowly to reinforce its weight.

Dove nods. "You're right. I do have William. But to

be honest it doesn't give me that much comfort." She pulls at a few pine needles from one of the trees. "We first kissed right over there. . . . It feels like a long time ago." *How is it that Max's birthday and everything that happened with Claire feels more recent? Maybe because it's still happening.* Dove sighs, knowing that she has pounds of fudge to bake for the dessert buffet later tonight, and sighs harder when she remembers how much Claire loves fudge. "She'll probably ask him to feed it to her."

Melissa looks at her like she's crazy. "What?"

Dove pats her back. "Never mind. Just getting ahead of myself. Back to the ball . . . how are the plans coming?" *Will I even get to go to the ball? God, now I really feel like Cinderella. And why would I? I'll be too busy packing for my flight the next day.*

"The plans are actually great. It's me that's the problem. Being at a fancy dress ball without a date isn't the end of the world, I'll grant you that." Melissa trudges forward, her boots crunching on the snow. "But it's not romantic. Especially when there's someone you want to go with . . ." She looks down, sliding her sunglasses over her eyes as the bright light reflects off the ground.

"Oh, we're calling him 'someone' now?" Dove laughs. "Between your boys and mine, we're a mess." Melissa nods, laughing, too. An announcement in French comes over the loudspeaker. "Oh—quick—it's the Super G. Let's hurry!"

Melissa picks up her pace, moving fast so she can secure a spot on the sidelines to watch someone—two someones—race at breakneck speeds. She takes one look over her shoulder at all the footsteps she's made in the snow. *I really have come a long way,* she thinks. *How is it possible that in such a short time I could go from having no love interests to being stuck between two impossible guys and one crazy job?* Taking the last couple of steps up to the sloping mountainside, she and Dove clamber to the front of the crowd, squeezing in so they'll be right at the finishing line. *Yes, lots of steps behind me,* she thinks as the announcer introduces the skiers. Gabe Schroeder. James Marks-Benton. *And lots of steps still to come.*

Dotted along the mountainsides like bright confetti are paparazzi, camera crews, reporters thrusting microphones this way and that, and many, many fans.

"Could there be more attractive females in a small area?" Dove asks, searching the crowd for Max. Having forgotten her sunglasses, she uses her hand to block the rays and frowns when she can't find him. Melissa watches her look. "It's not like I'm desperate to find him."

"Sure. Right." Melissa smirks.

"I only want to tell him about . . ." Dove stops herself from continuing.

Melissa's interest is piqued. "About what?"

Dove shrugs and shakes it off. "No. Nothing. Forget it."

Melissa wants to ask more but the race is about to start. Nudging her way to the very edge of the fan line, she wants to make sure she's as close to the finish as possible. *I remember reading that if you're right up front, the skiers are likely to hug you if they win. Or smile at you. Or spray you with champagne. Any of which would be fine.* As the first racer speeds down, she turns to Dove. "You think he'll see me here?" Melissa plants her boots firmly on the snow and fluffs out her signature curls.

"He'd have to be visually impaired to miss you." She smiles. "If James grabs anyone from the crowd, it's got to be you."

Fascinated with the incredible speed of the racers, the crowd *ooh*s and *ahh*s each time they swish by. Over the loudspeakers, an announcer comes on. "Translate for me?" Melissa asks Dove.

Dove keeps looking forward but explains, "She's saying that the Super G race is like a combination of downhill and giant slalom. It's viciously fast and physically demanding. Only top-form skiers can handle it." She grins at Melissa. "Hey—I know what you're thinking."

"What?" Melissa lets her eyes leave the hill just for a second so she can give a mischievous grin. "Get your mind out of the gutter. I'm not thinking about a certain someone's physical form—if that's what you're hinting at."

"Okay, whatever you say . . . but if you lean any farther into the guard rail you'll fall onto the course."

This makes Melissa take a small step back. "I really could be that person—I'm just that inept." She squints at the hill. "Oh my god—here's Gabe."

"Monsieur Gabriel Schroeder . . ." the announcer says, rattling off his height, weight, birthplace, and past achievements as he dodges the massive gates on his way through the course.

Despite waiting for James, Melissa's pulse speeds up as Gabe nears. His yellow-and-black jacket makes him appear beelike, buzzing through the gates until he comes to a fluid stop at the finish line. His skis aligned, he looks up at the clock, then right to the crowds.

"You do realize he just looked right at you," Dove says, squeezing Melissa's gloved hand.

Without breaking her plastered-on smile, Melissa speaks under her breath. "No, no. That wasn't at me. It must've been someone else."

As a reporter begins interviewing Gabe, he does one more glance over to the sidelines and waves to Melissa. This time, she's sure he meant the wave to go to her, since all eyes look her over, and the whispers begin.

"Great—now I'll be the subject of tabloid fodder."

Melissa blows air out of her mouth in a puff of white and feels a bump from behind.

"What's wrong with tabloid fodder? Who wouldn't want to be a celebrity for at least a day?" Charlie nudges between Dove and Melissa, out of breath. "God, I didn't miss the whole thing, did I?"

Melissa feels a chill, thinking about Charlie moving in on James, her easy beauty, how great she'd look in a paparazzi photograph compared to Melissa. "What brings you out of the chalet?"

"I love skeleton races—all speed and nothing else." Charlie slides a tube of pink gloss over her lips.

With the sun reflecting off Charlie's slick mouth, Melissa fights the urge to hand her fellow chalet girl a tissue. "Well, the skeleton's on the other side in an hour. It's still the Super G here. Sorry to disappoint."

Charlie frowns. "Oh, well." In her skintight black ski pants and bright pink turtleneck top, Charlie wraps her arms around herself and looks up the mountain. "Who'd I miss?"

Dove clears her throat. "A few skiers."

Charlie furrows her brow, peering over to the paparazzi section. "Isn't that Gabe Schroeder?" She looks impressed with the swarm of photographers around him.

"Yeah." Melissa feels possessive of him suddenly, and then wishes she had a carefree attitude about boys, one that would allow her to float around without worrying so much. "Actually, Gabe just did really well. I think *Sporting World* might put him on the cover."

Dove kicks Melissa's shin and she shrugs, mouthing, *What? It could be true. . . .*

Melissa is so busy watching Gabe navigate the throngs of fans and reporters that she misses the next announcement.

"Oh—here he comes!" Charlie looks like a schoolgirl, eyes forward as she waits.

"Monsieur James Marks-Benton . . ." the announcer says.

Melissa feels herself entranced, watching first the small, distant version of James in his orange-and-black racing outfit start the course. As he gets closer, she can make out his muscled legs, the way his body curves into and then away from each turn, propelling himself down the mountain toward the finish line.

With her heart slamming against her chest, Melissa can't help but smile as she checks the clock, certain James will win the whole competition. And maybe, just maybe, see her at the end mark. In one quick flash of black and orange, he whizzes around the last gate, nearly falls over a small patch of ice, and then finishes to the roar of the crowds.

"Oh, wow. Wow. That was incredible. . . ." Melissa feels so connected to him it's as though she raced, too. She's about to pick up her arm and wave to him, abandon her inhibitions and go for it, when she's shoved to the side. The crowd moves as a whole, swaying to the left and then back up again.

In the midst of all the hustle and bustle, Dove is shoved to the back, where she gives up and retreats toward the chalet to bake, and Melissa is knocked over. Even though she's on her butt on the ground in danger of being trampled, she laughs, feeling good about herself. *I've got the ball planned, an invite to a secret party, and I'm finally going to just break out and jump for joy around James. And all while being in pain.* She stands up, determined to shout and wave to him, to be the first person, aside from reporters, that he locks eyes with, but she's too late. As soon as she's upright, Melissa is hit head-on with a flash of bright pink and gloss—Charlie, not only near James, but hugging him full on. Tears sting her eyes and Melissa fights them off, suddenly feeling the cold air and the even colder feeling of having been usurped.

"Excuse me," says one of the tabloid photographers. "That girl—the gorgeous one with Mr. Marks-Benton. Do you know her?"

Melissa looks at Charlie, who is now getting a champagne spray from James. She winces as Charlie slings her arm around James and they pose for more pictures. "Yes. I do. Her name's Charlie."

"And she is?" The photographer jots notes onto a small pad.

Melissa knows the magazines will have a field day with the story. *I can see it now—Chalet Maid Wins Heart of Gold Medalist Skier. . . . I feel like I could throw up.* Then she thinks about the weekly celebrity mags she's read and what they always say. "She works at the resort—and they're just . . . friends."

10

Trays of hors d'oeuvres line every surface of the kitchen counters. Small silver serving dishes filled with Brie and cranberry puff pastries, trays of grilled asparagus wrapped in prosciutto, prawns in a curried ginger sauce and speared with rainbow peppers, and tea-sized smoked salmon sandwiches all wait to be served.

"This should do it." Dove takes the last selection from the oven.

"And that is?" Max stands in the doorway, looking as though he tumbled out of bed—all rumpled T-shirt, sweatpants, and bare feet.

Guess he didn't go to the races, thinks Dove as she

carefully plates the chicken satay skewers and mixes warm peanut sauce to drizzle on top. With a shudder she wonders if maybe Claire, too, missed out on the Super G and if maybe they spent the time together. Comfortably. In bed or somewhere like it. *If only he'd just come out with all his feelings at once, rather than having me guess at everything. Not that I'm the most expressive person, either.*

"This is chicken satay—a classic dipping food. With a spicy-sweet sauce."

"Spicy and sweet," Max brushes the hair from his eyes and just for a second looks cozy enough that Dove wants to hug him. "Just the way I like it."

"What a weird thing to say." Dove makes a face and turns back to the food, fussing over an asparagus that's come unwrapped. "Anyway, you'll have to excuse me—I have to put these out on the sideboard for when the team comes back."

"And then?" Max makes room for her to get by, and when Dove takes the first small tray, she squeezes past him, fully aware that her shoulder brushes his chest.

"And then I suspect I'll head into town." She doesn't look at Max as she brushes past again on her way to get the rest of the trays.

"What's in town?" Max begins to help with the trays, ferrying them from the kitchen to the living room and dining room.

"The Internet café, for starters." Dove doesn't add

that she's got an IM scheduled with William—their first in ages—and wonders why she wouldn't just tell that to Max.

Max nods. "I can take you, if you like."

Dove shrugs. "Could this be a display of gentlemanly help?"

"You can call it that." He pauses, his eyes searching her face for a response. "It's just a ride in—no strings attached."

"What does that mean?" Dove's heart kicks at her insides.

Max laughs, breaking the tension as Dove carries the last of the trays out and arranges a stack of blue paper napkins each trimmed in gold. "The room looks perfect. Really nice, Dove." He waits for her to finish. "So? Can I be your chauffeur?"

"Of all the things you could be, I guess my chauffeur is pretty innocuous." *Hard to believe I actually had a chauffeur not too long ago. All those nights, slinging through London, being the pampered one rather than the one doing the pampering.* Dove turns back to the spread of food she's shopped for, budgeted, and prepared all on her own, and feels good.

"Is that a yes?" Max rubs his pointer finger over his thumb—an old habit Dove still takes note of. She remembers sitting in the library with him, studying, right before they'd both been accepted to Oxford University, and how she'd grabbed his thumb to make him stop, and they'd wound up tangled on the hardwood floor.

Dove nods, cracking a smile. "Sure. What's the big deal about a lift into town, right?"

After she washes her hands and pats them dry on one of the kitchen cloths, she tugs at the hair on her forehead, smoothing it out. "It's a yes," she says softly. But Max has already gone to change and isn't there to see her very small, slightly devious grin.

Oh crap, oh crap, oh crap. Melissa tries her best to stay out of sight, ducking behind one of the resort vans, but it's too late. "Dodging Matron should be its own Olympic event," Melissa mutters as she faces the music and walks directly up to her superior, hoping to at least gain points for being up-front.

"Miss Forsythe." Matron, without a jacket and yet seemingly unfazed by the chill, has her hands clasped around her clipboard and her eyes set to penetrate even the slightest weakness.

"Matron . . ." Melissa changes her weight to her other foot, easing the ache of her ribs. "Glad I've found you. I wanted to let you know that the Winter Wonderland is all arranged. I took the liberty of ordering not only the decorations for inside, but as the theme is inspirational and set largely outside, I also had the factory in town create individual spheres." Melissa rambles on, spewing everything she's planned and taken care of all at once, hoping to impress and overwhelm Matron so she won't have many objections.

"Spheres?" Matron writes this down on her board.

"Yeah, you know, orbs. But these are huge. Imagine a carnival ride but made of clear glass. . . ."

"Glass?"

Melissa coughs from way down in her throat out of nervousness. "Maybe not glass. Plastic? Anyway, each one could probably fit two people and they'd be illuminated from the bottom, so they'd glow. Like an iridescent snowball."

This last image resonates with Matron and she stops writing to look at Melissa and listen. "And?"

"And the electricians have already met with the kitchen staff, because I wanted a . . ." She pauses, momentarily losing her footing. "I thought it would be fun and different if we had a conveyor belt. . . ."

"That sounds rather industrial." Matron's mouth forms a straight line.

"No—wait. That came out wrong. What I mean is . . ." Melissa risks being yelled at and grabs Matron's clipboard. She draws what she means. "See? Small tables, all glowing with that interior light, and food on top. Only the tables can move. The resort's mechanics and electrical crew said they could do it. . . ."

"Really?"

Melissa nods and gently hands the clipboard back to Matron. "They said they'd look upon the job as a challenge." She sighs and smiles. "Plus, I told the head electrician that his daughter could be the snow princess."

Matron rattles her pen against the clipboard and casts a doubtful eye. "And that is?"

"Just a title. She can be the one to start the festivities—in the miniature hot-air balloon over the ice lake."

Matron looks transformed—she claps her hands and smiles. "I knew it. I knew you had it in you, even with a broken ankle or whatever it was you had."

"Have." Melissa briefly relives the skiing, the dare from Gabe, the falling, the massive wipeout, and feels annoyed all over again that she was swayed into the jump. "I *still* have it—broken ribs." Melissa pats her sides, momentarily distracted from Matron's enthusiasm by a large herd of people moving toward the Main House.

"I do hope you're getting rest." She writes something down. As she continues to write Melissa begins to wonder what she could possibly have missed. Matron checks over her shoulder, noticing the sizeable crowd by the Main House. "The paparazzi never loses interest, do they?"

Like I'm so experienced with cameras flashing and microphones protruding. Without knowing what to say,

Melissa wills herself not to think of Charlie and the supreme confidence or cruelty that made her jump all over James. Melissa thinks of her largely sleepless nights and her aching heart, not to mention her ribs, and shrugs. "All part of the job, I guess." She tries to sneak a look at Matron's clipboard. *I hope she likes all my plans. I'm sure she does. And now that they're basically in place, I can chill for the first time in days.* "Anything I didn't answer?"

Matron goes back to her straight-lined mouth and shakes her tightly bunned head. "All set, it seems." She jots one more thing down and circles it.

Melissa smiles, satisfied. "Great."

"All except for one thing . . ." Matron points to the writing on her board. "Where exactly are you going to fit the ballroom into this outdoor extravaganza?"

What? Crap oh crap oh crap. Melissa's mouth drops open. "Ballroom? I thought . . . it was, you know, a dance. And we could all . . ." She looks out to the lake. "Dance on the lake?" In her mind it had seemed beautiful and serene, romantic, as if everyone had been transported back in time.

Matron crosses her arms and shifts her stance, clearly wanting to deal with the crowd overtaking the Main House. "Miss Forsythe—Melissa—this is a luxury resort. The Winter Wonderland Ball is covered in *Tatler, Hello!, Vogue, Vanity Fair*, and every major newspaper. Royalty from the Baltics, all of Europe, South America, and Asia will be here, along with all of our other guests. How exactly did you think you would fit them all onto our quaint ice pond?"

Feeling stupid and foolish, Melissa looks at the ground, studying the grains of sand and salt scattered to melt the ice on the pavement. In a small voice she says, "I don't know."

Matron taps her shoulder in order to make eye contact. "Well, you're a creative thinker. And clearly you can handle pressure. I'm sure you'll sort it out." Matron starts to walk away. "Six hundred guests—minimum."

"By myself?" Melissa clenches her stomach, then winces. "I thought maybe you'd . . ."

"I," Matron starts, "have to contend with the huddled masses."

And just like that, Melissa finds herself alone with a new pile of headaches coming on. Six hundred guests? With the ability to dance at the same time, should they desire? While still having access to the food, music, and drinks? No wonder an outdoor event hadn't been attempted. *I'm a big, big fool.* Melissa shakes her head at herself. Way off by the Main House's front door, she sees Charlie's recognizable head of tousled strawberry locks. *Of course she's with James. Charlie and James are part of a champagne-soaked group to which I clearly don't belong.* Melissa shakes her head again. *Yes, I'm a big fool.*

D & M—

This is a panoramic shot of me and my new clan of beach dwellers. We call ourselves that because we're in the surf every chance we get. Of course, I'm not fully ditching my hosting duties (I did land a gold reservation at the elite course by the sugar mill, which gave me major points), but the soft air and salty boys do make for big-time distractions.

Did you get my last postcard?

I haven't heard from either of you, which makes me wonder if you're getting any of the cards I've sent! I'm using the overnight service here (charge it to my guests, of course) but haven't heard back. Hope you guys aren't pissed at me or anything for leaving. If you were here, you'd get why. . . .

Harley

11

Town is abuzz with talk of a storm. The church bells haven't yet sounded their warning—six quick rings in close succession—but the skies tell everyone to be careful.

"I heard five feet."

"Three."

"Eight—easy. Remember the storm of La Rein a few years ago?"

Melissa sits with her second cup of café au lait, swirling a thick shortbread biscuit into the creamy drink as she wonders for the fiftieth time what she can do to solve the Winter Wonderland problem.

"They call it CBs." Gabe sits across from her, slapping

the table with his gloves enough so that it wobbles and sends a splash of au lait onto Melissa's lap. "Chalet blues."

"Why do you do that?" She looks cross, her brows furrowed, her cheeks pink from the interior heat of the coffeehouse. Built originally as a tavern, the place is cozy and set way back from the town. *I thought I'd be away from everyone here. . . . But I guess trouble finds me twenty-four/seven.*

"Do what?" Gabe looks as her as though he's done nothing. Ever charming, he's recognized by a bunch of people in the café, who whisper about him in French until he smiles at them and nods. A group of girls giggles and wants to ask for his autograph but they are clearly too shy.

Melissa swipes a napkin from the counter, blots her pants and top, and shows him the evidence. "This. Spill things. You make messes. . . ."

Gabe's silvery blond hair is slightly matted in the back, the mark from his glasses clear above his ears. "So you're still pissed about the rope-swing thing?"

They look at each other over the small round table, the clink of cutlery and the smell of mulled cider around them. "No. It's not that. You didn't make me do it—you just encouraged me." Melissa slumps her chin into her hand.

"Then what is it? Why am I such a bad guy?"

Melissa shakes her head, her tight ringlets moving

with the motion. "It's not you." Melissa starts off slowly but then her words develop a velocity akin to Gabe's racing. "It's . . . I thought I had everything figured out for the ball but I don't." Melissa's mind starts to gain speed, too, and she finds herself spilling more than she intended. ". . . And then I thought that maybe I had a chance in hell of having my affections returned but it's so not the case I don't know who I was kidding. I should just pack up, since I'm unqualified to be the perfect host, and go back to Australia. I mean, it's summer there now. . . ." She looks at Gabe, whose plush mouth is curved into a grin as he watches her. "Oh—and I didn't . . . I never even said congratulations to you for your races today."

"I didn't win." Gabe bristles when he says it, and begins folding a napkin into halves, then fourths, then eighths.

"But you competed. And did well. You tried and so maybe you didn't win—but you did great."

Gabe raises his eyebrows, his teeth white against his lips, his look soft. "I could say the same for you."

They sit there, in comfortable quiet, shooting the folded-up napkin back and forth into goals made out of their fingers, until the light shifts outside. "Oh, it's going to come down out there." Gabe flicks his fingers toward the window. "Massive."

"Everyone's overreacting. Last time they said this we only got a foot. Maybe a foot-plus." Melissa peers out the window and up to the sky, coated in thick white-blue clouds that resemble quilted blankets. "Just a pleasant holiday-week sprinkling . . ."

"Whatever." Gabe takes the opportunity to score a goal with the napkin and cheers for himself. "So . . ." He looks away from her and clears the plates and cups. "Who's the guy?"

Flustered, Melissa makes a coughing sound. "Who? What do you mean?"

"The unreturned affection that you spoke of. Who is it?" Gabe looks at her, probing with his gaze.

I can't figure him out. Does he think I like James still? Or someone new, some random guy on the slopes? Melissa and Gabe lock eyes. She remembers seeing him for the first time, how the jolt buzzed through her, and then how when she saw him again with James, she didn't know where to look first. *How do you tell your old crush, the crush that came to fruition last week, that it's his best friend that you more than like?* "It's no one you know."

Gabe looks funny, his mouth slack. Then Melissa realizes, it's not funny, just relief that has washed over Gabe's face. "Well, let me know if you want a reference. . . ." He smiles cheekily. "And don't let him give you any shit. If you want, you can bring your little friend to the—you know . . ."

"Ze zecret affair?" Melissa puts on a French accent and hints at the party.

Gabe nods. He crumples the football-napkin and flings it at her. "You're pretty cool when you're not defensive and brittle."

"And you're pretty kind when you're not a sleazebag ho-bag womanizer."

"Shake?" Gabe holds out his hand and Melissa grasps it, laughing, before she heads out into the sky's pale light.

"You've got to check it out." Max motions with his arm for Dove to follow him.

"I thought I was just getting a ride into town. . . ." Dove tucks the edges of her multicolored scarf into her jacket. William gave her the scarf and it's really, now that she looks at it, not her style, but she wears it, anyway, because of the intent.

"You will get a ride. I just want to show you my Christmas present first." Max pulls on a black ski cap.

Dove checks out Max from the side as they walk past the Main House, in back of the electrical and building-supply sheds, onto the frozen ground near the stables. *You'd think people would look funny with hats on,* she thinks, *but instead they just look more intense. Or at least, Max does. All bright eyes, intent gaze. His mouth is*—she cuts off her thoughts once she checks the time. "Not to rain on your present parade, but I have to go."

Max stops in his tracks. "I know, I know. You've got your romantic Internet conversation planned." He's semi-joking but holds up his hands to show he means no harm. "I have no intention of coming between you and your . . ."

Boyfriend. Dove repeats the word in her mind but lets out only a puff of white breath. "So what's this exciting gift, anyway? I thought your parents were more of the leather-bound books and silver flask set."

"Yes, just like yours." Max nudges Dove back to her own family, their quiet holidays spent tucked in by the fireside, opening stacks of gifts by themselves.

Dove sticks out her tongue. "Do you know how pathetic it is? We write thank-you notes to one another—right there. You open a gift, barely have time to look at it, and immediately sit down and write a thank-you note on personalized stationery."

"You write thank-yous to your parents?"

"And my sisters." Dove sighs, relieved she's not there this year, that she's free to be off on her own. Still, there was something cozy about being at her parents' house on New Year's. They'd always leave and she'd make dinner for a few friends. "Did you come last year?"

Max doesn't need to ask where. "You made the tenderloin, with that currant sauce."

Dove nods. *It's nice he remembers. But it doesn't mean anything.* "Okay—so two seconds and then you'll drive me to town?"

Max smirks. "Two seconds, yes. Drive? No."

He points behind the stables and Dove goes to check it out. "Don't tell me you're trotting me into town? I like horses, but I think the time for Jane Austen rides is—"

"It's not a horse, though the idea of a snow-filled ride sounds kind of fun." Max takes a few long strides and pulls a thick cream-colored cover from a heap on the ground.

He tries not to stare at Dove, but she can feel his gaze rest on her just a few seconds too long, his hands linger on her shoulder only the slightest bit longer than normal, but enough to give her chills.

"Snow? You really think we're going to get some this time? It seems like every other day there's some warning or announcement about heavy accumulation."

Max shrugs. "Yeah, probably nothing. So . . . what do you think?" He shows off the present as though he's displaying a game show prize. "It's brand-new. State-of-the-art hybrid snowmobile with silent motor."

Dove watches Max's face. *For some reason I thought he'd be all jaded about gifts, as though nothing anyone could give him would be cool.* "This is awesome. Even though I'm more of a cross-country nature kind of person . . . it looks fun."

"Hop on!" Max pats the seat and hands her a helmet.

Dove shakes her head. "Oh, no way. I thought you

were just showing me. . . . I have to get into town for real."

"Do you know how backed up traffic is right now?" Max slides his helmet on. He presses a button and makes it so they can talk through small speakers in the helmets. "Trust me, this will be faster than driving. Everyone's trying to vacate town just in case we do get that blizzard."

Dove checks her watch, her heart racing with not wanting to miss William's IM. *I just want to see him. If I could just see Will it would be so much easier. All of this, it wouldn't matter.* "Can you really get me to the café in eighteen minutes?"

"Twelve. I'll get you there in twelve. We can take Gooseneck Gorge."

"Isn't that kind of steep?" Dove climbs on in back of Max and looks for something to hold on to that isn't him.

"It's a little treacherous, but it's the fastest way in. You all set?" He turns to check on her and she nods as he starts up the miraculously quiet engine.

With no handles, no grips, Dove has no choice but to lean a little into Max and put her hands on his waist, hoping he knows it, too, doesn't mean anything.

12

"*Allez! Allez!* Attention!" The French voices, filled with concern and haste, urge Melissa to keep moving on the sidewalk. Past the grocery where she stocks up, past the café where she sat with Gabe, she dawdles near the news agent, wondering if all the fuss over the weather is worth it.

I mean, it's snow, for god's sake. And we're in a snow resort. How big a deal could it possibly be?

"I'm closing early," the news agent tells her, already packing up the day's papers and bringing them inside the small shop. Melissa watches the man, knowing she needs to get back to the chalet and resume her hosting duties, but also troubled by the lack of having presented Matron with a perfect plan for the ball. "Are you buying anything?"

Melissa shoves her hands deeper into her pockets, fending off the chilly air, and gazes at the foreign papers. World news from Rome, Paris, India, New York, and none of it mentioning the massive snow everyone predicts. Studying the sky, she asks the news agent, "Is all this for real?"

His accent thick, he responds with a huff, as if she's crazy to doubt the power of a potential storm. "You never know until it's 'appening.

" 'Ere." The news agent thrusts a paper at her before gathering the rest to bring inside. "It's the afternoon edition. Won't sell them all now—not like this." He glances at the thickening clouds. "You can have for free a look at what's 'appening."

With her bare hand instantly cold, she grips the paper, planning to get rid of it as soon as the man's inside and it's polite enough to chuck it. Not that she's not interested in the greater events of the Trois area, but right now she has other things on her mind. Then, just as she's about to try to invigorate herself to make a move and head back to the chalet, she stops short.

There, on the front of the afternoon edition of the paper, is enough to make her lose her breath. "L'amour," she reads, the word in capital letters, which only highlight the photograph underneath. There, fixed on the page, is Charlie, doting, her head on James's shoulder, his arm wrapped protectively around her. She's looking at the camera's lens; he's gazing at her. *Crap oh crap, oh crap. He's so into her. Check out the way he's unable to break away—not even for a major photo op.* Melissa shakes her head. A glutton for punishment, she doesn't throw the thing out, but instead takes it with her and goes back to the café. After ordering an urgent double hot-chocolate swirl in a glass, she sits nursing the remedy and reading the parts of the French she can understand. First she reads *amour vrai*—"true love," and has to stop herself from spitting out her drink. Then some ski info about the race and . . .

"He loves her? True love?" Melissa traces the word *copine* with her finger, wishing she didn't know it means "girlfriend." *So she's his girlfriend. It's official. This sucks.* She keeps studying the picture, the angle of Charlie's chin on James' body, the way his fingers seem to be pulling at her like he can't get her close enough. It's only when she sees the word *fiançailles* that Melissa pushes the paper as far from her as possible, loses interest in her drink, and puts her head in her hands. *Fiancée? Engaged?*

A tap on the shoulder surprises Melissa, as does the ringing of the church bells.

"You feel asleep," the café owner says.

"I fell asleep?"

"Feel, yes."

Not wanting to argue about the wording, Melissa stands up, both feeling asleep and having fallen asleep, and feels her stomach churn with the sound of the bells. What did it say in the informational packet that was handed out last week when she first got to Les Trois? Melissa remembers the small print under the heading *Weather Difficulties. Les Trois is located in a valley and therefore likely to have heavy snowfall. In the long run this gives us enviable conditions for skiing and boarding, but in the short term, it may be cause for alarm. Should there be a warning issued, be advised to return to your chalet immediately and wait for word form the office.*

In English, she asks the café owner, "Is that the warning bell?"

The café owner, all serious-looking and businesslike in her manner as she readies to close the café, shakes her head. "We already had the warning. This one—this is to say we are *in* the storm."

Melissa does a quick check outside. "Storm?" *Fine, so I'm from Australia, where we're not exactly snow mavens, but there's hardly a flake falling from the sky.* She drops a few Euros onto her table, tucks the paper with its horrible photo in her jacket so she can moan over it with Dove later, and steps again onto the cobblestone streets to start once and for all back to the resort.

Once outside, she thinks about what Gabe said. *Prepare for it.* She can hear phrases like *seasonal frequencies of intense snowfall episodes* and *storm path migration* ringing through her ears as the flakes begin to fall. Phrases from the chalet informational packet she read when she first arrived at Les Trois, but it all seems unreal and long ago. Dreamy at first, Melissa spins around in the snow, catching a few flakes on her eyelashes and then on her tongue. *It's romantic, really, provided you have someone to be with. Which I don't.*

"I feel like I'm in an advertisement for . . ." Dove pauses. "What'd you say the name of this thing is?"

Max's elbow touches Dove's arm as he responds. "Marchese Belloch 2000. Best money can buy." He lets go of the steering mechanism with one hand to pat the side of the snowmobile as if it's a pony. His hand grazes her thigh but he instantly whisks it away.

Dove watches the scenery glide by all in a wash of the first few flakes that have started falling. Over the hum of the engine she thinks she hears something. "Was that a clanging noise?"

Max shrugs and turns his head to show he's listening, but then shakes it off. "Didn't hear anything. Must be the hydraulics."

Dove tucks her chin farther into her red neck warmer

and hopes for the hundredth time that she'll make it in time for the IM with William. In her mind she has visions of how it will go—with him telling her how much he misses her, leading off with how miserable he's been without her, and then maybe following up with plans for what they'll do once she arrives on New Year's Day. *I'll ask him about Harley, of course—way too curious to find out if he's met her yet.* Dove swallows. *It's weird that we haven't heard from her. Or maybe it isn't—I mean, mail takes forever and we don't have e-mail access and . . . I trust him, though. Even if Harley is wild and hot and exactly the kind of girl you don't want bumping into your boyfriend on the beach in a string bikini. At least she knows me and could bring my name up.* "Wait—I heard it again—I think those were bells."

"Maybe someone's getting married?" Max points to a far-off field. "See that? Over the hill? I think one of my professors lives there. Or—vacations nearby or something."

"Weird coincidence." Dove looks at the compact farmhouse set back from the paths and trees, all cozy among the falling snow. "Do you miss it?"

Max turns, his helmet making him look like a futuristic bug. "Miss what?"

"School."

Max turns back to the path, zooming up a steep hill, past a mound of old snow and veering left to avoid a patch of thick ice. He doesn't respond.

Dove wants to check her watch but can't or she'll lose her grip on Max and fall off. "I have to admit," she says, trying to wash over the school question, which clearly didn't sit well, "this is a pretty sweet ride."

"Better be."

"Oh yeah? Why?"

Max puts on the brakes, slowing the whole mobile to a stop. He puts his hand on Dove's knee, then thinks better of it and takes it away. Dove thinks it's the kind of touch—gentle but firm—that stays with you after it's over. "No reason—just—it's my big Christmas gift this year, so . . ." His voice fades out as he starts up again. Town is in view now, just over one more hill and beyond a big field.

"I swear I hear bells." Dove nudges Max now with each clang, and her heart rate picks up as the snowflakes do. *Maybe someone's getting married in town.* Rather than the gentle, almost dreamlike, flow they had a few minutes before, the sky seems to be opening up, spilling the contents of a sack of rice, or a pillow, all over the ground, making the snowmobile work harder. *Good thing we're in this vehicle, I guess,* Dove thinks. *Although it's kind of an odd purchase, seeing as Max is only here on vacation. What will he do to get it home? Probably sell it. Or just leave it.* Dove shakes her head at the thought of all that wasted money.

"Watch out!" Dove grabs hold of Max's waist, maybe

a little too tightly, as they nearly hit a snow-covered rock.

Max veers quickly to the right to avoid a boulder, causing Dove to giggle out of nervousness. "Oh my god—this is a little too much for me."

Max stops the snowmobile and takes off his helmet. Steam rises from his hair into the cold air, flakes dotting his lips and face. "How many bells do you think you heard?"

Dove pauses, suddenly putting the snow together with the sound and realizing the clangs were warning bells, the kind she'd been advised about when she vacationed at Les Trois. "Enough that we shouldn't be out here . . ." She checks her watch. Five minutes. "Think I could walk into town?"

Max gives her an annoyed look. "We're talking major snow event here and you're still hoping to get into some café to chitchat?"

"Don't make it sound stupid." Dove's voice is defensive. *How dare he make fun of me or belittle my IM with William.* "I mean, thanks for the ride and everything, but . . ."

Max sighs, thinking, and pulls at his hair. His cheeks are flushed. "Considering the snowfall, we have enough power in this thing to go into town or back, but not both."

"I thought you said this is the best on the market."

Max shoots her a look. "It *is*. But it doesn't change the fact that if you calculate the rate of the snow and factor that into the distance into town and back to Les Trois . . ."

"Okay, Captain Math."

Max rolls his eyes. "You have a better idea?"

Dove stands up, unstraddling the snowmobile and breaking away from Max's body. Instantly she's colder than she was next to him, and aware of wanting to be back with him, but she's determined to get into town. "I'm not ready to turn around. I want to walk."

"Fine—suit yourself." Max crosses his arms over his chest and waits for Dove to move, which she does, finally taking a few steps toward town.

Five minutes later, she's up to her knees in a combination of old and new snow, her whole body shaking with cold. *Hot chocolate. Sun. William in a bathing suit. William on the beach. William rubbing sunblock everywhere. Nice warm things. Not like here. In this frozen wasteland.* Ahead, the lights in town are flickering as though it's already pitch-black.

"You realize, of course, that town will be closed. Except for emergency vehicles and the hardware store, it's done." Dove hears Max's voice, the low hum of the snowmobile catching up to her, but refuses to turn around. "Remember that year we were twelve?" Max eggs her on with the memory. "The Easter blizzard? Kept the roads closed for a week." Max laughs. "We were stranded at the resort. I seem to recall you and I managed to fill the indoor pool with—"

"Rubber ducks. Five thousand of them." Dove gives a conciliatory look and wrinkles her nose. "You think this storm'll be that bad?" She calculates, realizing if it is, she'd miss her flight to Nevis altogether.

Max watches her face, then looks up at the flowing snow. Catching her eye, he knows she needs to hear it will all work out, that she won't be stranded. "It'll be fine. One bad night, maybe, and then they'll get the crews out to clear."

Dove sighs, relieved. "Good." She lifts her boot up from the snow and stomps. "So, what does a girl have to do to get a lift somewhere?"

"Nothing. Just ask." Max pats the snowmobile and makes room for her, smiling at her the way he did when he first asked her to dance.

Trying to ignore her disappointment at missing the IM with William, Dove is aware of the ramifications this might bring. *What if William just thinks I'm blowing him off? What if he takes it as a lack of interest? What if he were the one not to show?* "Whoa. Talk about snow." Dove has to leave behind her thoughts of the tropics and her boyfriend to deal with the blinding snow that's covering everything. "What do we do?"

Max latches his helmet and warms up the engine.

"The only thing we can. Try and start back and see where we wind up."

Dove grimaces in her helmet. "That sounds rather undefined. I mean, isn't there someone to call or shout to?"

Max tilts his helmet so it clanks onto Dove's. Through their visors they look at each other, his eyes glinting. "Hang on and have faith."

13

The sting from the wind and sleeting snow is nothing compared to the harsh reality of yet another daily newspaper's account of the budding romance between James and Charlie. LES DEUX AMANTS. Melissa reads the headline, squinting through the snow that appears to be piling up every second around her ankles. *The two lovers? Who says* lovers *anymore? What an annoying term.* Melissa makes a face at the words, feeling all over again the now-familiar tug at her heart, the emotional bruising that comes from liking someone who doesn't like you back.

She bites her lip as she looks at the photo from the race—Charlie's arm around James—and then she can't look any longer. Not because it hurts too much, which it does, but because looking at anything for too long is impossible.

"Oh my god!" Melissa blurts out into the snowy air, aware that talking to herself won't really increase the likelihood that James or anyone else will find her irresistible. *I have to go somewhere, find a place to wait out the worst of this before trying to get back*. Melissa shoves the anxiety about Matron's dance-floor concerns and her love woes aside and thinks three words:

Gabe was right.

Town has emptied out. The last few people retreat to their apartments in town, or brave the walk to the nearby hotel, but no cars move. Only the bright flashing from the snowplows and the incessant bells from the church give signs of life. Melissa suddenly knows what it's like to be really, truly alone.

I'm deserted. Or I've deserted myself. She tucks her chin into her jacket, wishing she'd brought more clothing—or taken Gabe's warnings more seriously and retreated to Les Trois while she still could. Her boots slide on the ice forming along the cobblestones, and her lips and cheeks feel wind burned. Determined, Melissa shoves her hands deep into her pockets and walks, knowing that if she stops for too long she'll get frostbite or stuck. And since she didn't tell anyone where she was going, no one knows to look for her away from the resort. No one except Gabe.

I could freeze out here. Or vanish. Melissa's heart races when she thinks about becoming her own headline. With her right hand she braces against the brick building; her left hand feels something in her pocket—a receipt? A candy? She pulls it out—a folded business card from the supply store. *That's it! The factory.* Melissa envisions the large doorways there and figures that at the very least she'll be able to find shelter in the tunnel that marks the entryway.

She shuffles down the street, leaning into the buildings so she doesn't fall, so she has something solid backing her up, and starts off.

"You're crazy!"

"Not as much as you think." Max laughs, removing his helmet and sticking it under his arm as he reaches to knock on the door in front of him.

"You can't just go into some random person's house and demand entry, as in, 'We'd like to come in—now!' " Dove blocks his knocking by elbowing his side. Reaching for his hands feels too flirty. Too couply. Too everything.

Max raises his eyebrows and gestures to the feet of snow, the whiteout conditions, and stomps his foot on the porch, where his boot leaves a small mound of flakes. "I don't think this counts as crazy. Maybe survivalist." He gets a gleam in his eyes. "We're on an adventure."

Dove smiles at him, rolling her eyes at his host-of-a-travel-show excitement, but feels it, too. It's different, fun, daring to be caught in a storm with a friend, a guy who isn't afraid. Dove imagines telling the story of their adventure. *We were completely snowed in—we were stuck—we were . . . too many* wes. *I couldn't explain it to William. Maybe I'll just have to relay it to Melissa and skip William altogether. After all, he may not even want to hear anything from me after the IM debacle.*

Max knocks loudly on the door before Dove can stop him again. Cracking up, she reaches for his wrist—not the hand, just the safe area of his jacket cuff—and stops him too late.

"You realize, of course, that we could be standing on the porch of a killer hiding out from the police? Or a deranged old woman who poisons the tea she's about to offer us? Or a creepy old skier who lost a gold medal and takes it out on unsuspecting passersby? Or a vampire?" Dove jokes but feels her chest heavy with worry. "I mean, no one knows where we are."

Dove turns her face up to Max. He stares at her, mouth locked in a half grin, and nods. Behind the howling wind and thick door, they can hear footsteps. Dove backs up a few feet, wishing she could grab Max's wide hand as the front door starts to open.

"The word *desolate* is the only one springing to mind," Melissa mutters as she pounds the door to the factory and wishes for the hundredth time that she were back at the chalet, or on a beach, anywhere warm, and preferably somewhere with another human being.

In an instant, she gets one of her wishes. From the intercom on the side of the gate, a muffled voice: "I'll buzz you in—take the side stairs."

Side stairs? Melissa shrugs. She never knew there were side stairs, but like she's gone through a magical porthole in a children's book, as soon as she steps in the courtyard she sees on the far left a small archway with steep steps. *This will be fine—I can wait out the storm here with the salespeople, and then head back to Les Trois and deal with Matron's wrath later.* Melissa has visions of entering the main storage room upstairs and finding a cozy floor picnic set up; maybe the workers would have assembled some chocolate bars or cheese and crackers, and made a fire in the previously abandoned marble fireplace. She allows a small smile to creep onto her face, and then winces when she feels the ache from the cold.

As soon as she's up the stairs the wind quiets and finally Melissa can hear herself think, hear her footsteps as she enters the main room. Just as she remembers, all sorts of strange and beautiful items adorn the walls and floor. Glowing signs from old hotels, a mobile made of sparkling stars, a basketball hoop, a jumble of skis and poles that instantly reminds her of the race today and James, and then—before she can stop herself—that image of Charlie with her arm around him. *That should be me.* Melissa frowns and then looks for the picnicking staff, the blaze of a fire, some company other than her thoughts.

"Welcome, welcome." The salesman beckons Melissa to the tally room, where his immaculate bookkeeping records are stacked in rows.

"Thanks—it's freezing and I managed to get myself stuck in town." Melissa's jacket is soaked nearly through; her boots drip onto the floor. "Sorry."

"Not a problem. Back about a decade ago we had fifteen skiers in here overnight—turned into quite the festive scene." He takes a jacket from the back of his desk chair and slides it on.

"Fifteen? That sounds fun." She almost looks around to see if that scene will recreate itself, but she hears no noises, no clinking glasses, no laughter. When she sees him put his black hat on, she starts to panic. "Wait—you're not leaving, are you? I mean, I need to stay, I don't have anywhere to . . ."

"Oh, it's fine. You can stay here until tomorrow or until the snow eases up, whichever comes first. But I . . ." He starts out of the room and toward the exit. "I have to run—I'm a backup snowplow driver and—" He reaches out to hand her a slip of paper. "It's my home number.

Just in case you have a problem." He peers behind Melissa to look out the arched window. "I might not be there for a few hours, but . . ."

"Thanks." Melissa nods at the snow and pockets the paper. *So much for the company. So much for not feeling completely deserted.* "At least I'll be warm."

Once the echoes from his footsteps fade, the silence creeps in as Melissa tries her best not to think about every horror flick she's ever seen, every movie in which a young woman just like her is somehow left alone in an unfamiliar setting.

Dove's heart pounds as the front door of the cottage swings open. "We'll be a headline—*Two Brits Bumble into Bad Situation, Get Beheaded.*" She whispers this to Max.

"Then someone will make it into a movie." Max smirks and does his signature sideways glance. Dove feels her stomach clench the way it did when he gave her the same look across the lecture room back at school. "Remember: Adventure is good."

The door opens to reveal a tall man in a heavy cloak, wielding an ax. Dove fights the urge no longer and grabs Max's hand. Their gloves collide more than grasp, though, so she drops it and tries to bring to mind a happy thought. The snapshot of her and William on the mountainside in the summer. *Green foliage, lush leaves. How'd I go from there to here? I can see him now, tan the way he was in the summer, but located on the sand, staring at the ocean. Or being rubbed down by some vixen. Some vixen who could be Harley. She said she'd write, but she hasn't.* Dove sighs. *Not that I've written to her, either.* Dove shudders picturing Harley's cool moves, her subtle ways of latching on. Then Dove refocuses and gets chills all over again when she sees again the ax-wielding man in front of her.

With one hand on the ax's handle, the other on the door, the man asks, "Would you like to come in? You must be freezing."

"Um, that's okay. We're just . . ." Dove stammers, thinking that being cold is better than being anywhere near the ax.

"Sure thing." Max glides through the doorway as though there's nothing wrong with this picture, and when he notices Dove's hesitations, pulls her inside.

The man with the ax closes—and locks—the door behind them.

14

"What do you do in a situation like this?" Melissa says aloud, figuring that talking into the air doesn't make her crazy, especially in this situation, and since hearing a voice—anyone's voice—is comforting. "Answer: Make the most of it."

Melissa finds the thermostat, cranks it up, and when the hot rush of air escapes from the floor vents, she stands on it until she feels herself relax. Finally warm and dealing with the random nature of her evening, she investigates the premises further.

"Nice dress!" she says aloud as she flings through a rack of ornate costumes: a hot-pink floor-length dress in

the style of Little Bo Peep, three matching judge's uniforms, several angels complete with glitter and wings, and a shiny red satin devil with a pointed tail. Figuring she has nothing better to do, Melissa slides out of her damp jeans and top and wriggles first into one of the angel outfits.

Um, not quite. She turns in the mirror and looks herself over. *If I were maybe taller or shaped differently or somehow more . . . angelic . . . this wouldn't be so bad. But as it is . . .* Melissa shakes her head, strips down again, and returns the white costume back to the rack. *I'm not being a judge. No way. I have to do that too much already—deciding the ball theme, figuring out if Dove's doing the right thing, if I am . . . no thanks.* She passes by the judge outfits and goes for the ridiculous dress.

Inching into the crinkly pink fabric, Melissa laughs. *This is worse than my sister's maid-of-honor dress—and that was unbelievable.* Puffy sleeves, fitted corset in frills of turquoise and white, a full hoop skirt with trails and loops of ribbons, and a bonnet. *Gotta have the hat,* Melissa figures, and slides it on her head, still laughing. *If only Dove could see me now—she'd have a fit.* Melissa goes to the full-length mirror and turns around to gawk at the sheer misfortune of the costume. *You couldn't pay me enough to wear this in public. Unless it was a dare. Then . . . maybe.*

In the three-way mirror, there are three Melissas looking silly but having a blast, three Melissas who have temporarily forgotten the stress of finding a dance floor for the masses, the day-to-day dealings of her job, and mainly, who have for now put aside the memory of Charlie and James on the cover of every newspaper in town.

Melissa bows to herself, imagining she's at the winter gala, and then nearly falls over with the width of the hoop skirt and the ruffles. "Am I the biggest freak in the world, or what?" she says, and shakes her head, which causes the bonnet to slip over her eyes.

When she pushes it back, her body ripples with surprise. She is not alone in the mirror. There, along with three of her own silly reflections, is James. Melissa's insides immediately do twists and turns and she wishes—wholeheartedly—that there really were three of him, and finally, enough to go around.

Using his ax as a sort of cane, the man leads Dove and Max over to a small sitting area. On the floor is a braided rug in muted reds and oranges that highlight the colors of the fire glowing in the deep fireplace.

"Please have a seat." The man gestures to the worn leather chairs nestled in between stacks of books. Max immediately takes a seat after removing his coat. Dove stays standing, ready to bolt, her jacket zipped. Her gloves drip onto the rug, and the quiet is so intense she can hear the small droplets hit the braids.

What the hell is Max's problem? Dove bites her lip, debating whether she should make a run for the door and brave the snow or face the ax and potentially poisoned cookies and tea the man offers. "The tea is wonderful—made from persimmons and ginger."

"Didn't a Shakespeare play end with a poisoned persimmon?" The question escapes Dove's mouth before she reels it back in.

Max raises his eyebrows. "Don't look at me—I'm not the best Shakespeare scholar."

The man holds the ax in both hands, his eyes gleaming. "Doesn't this have the makings of a play, though? Two lost travelers—young, lovers perhaps—find themselves lost in the frigid winds of a storm in the alps. . . ."

"And they stumble into a . . ." Max continues, seemingly immune to the mention of him and Dove being lovers.

"Into a terrifying situation where they end up hacked to bits." Dove says the words fast, then makes a move for the door.

The man with the ax begins to laugh—first a small chuckle, then a full belly laugh that spreads to his entire body so much that he puts the ax down and shakes his head. "Is that what you think?" he asks when Dove's about to try to unlock the door. Afraid to say yes, Dove fiddles with the multifaceted lock and glares at Max. "Is that what you've been doing, Max? Spreading stories, fables about me?"

Dove continues to try to unhook the heavy latch until she realizes the man called Max by his name without having been introduced.

"To what do I owe this honor?" Melissa asks, attempting to feel dignified despite her bonnet, hoop skirt, and frills.

James swipes his ski hat from his head and looks down at his feet, as though he's embarrassed to be seen here. "Ski patrol called in reinforcements to clear any remaining pedestrians. I'm not supposed to 'endanger myself,' but . . . a bunch of us . . ." He shrugs and begins to take in his surroundings—the large props, the costumes. "I barely got here. The snowmobile broke down—some plow driver gave me a ride in the rest of the way."

Melissa begins to feel something—annoyed? *How can I be annoyed at him?* "But why are you here, in this place—with me?" Instantly she wishes she could remove the *with me* from her question. *But seriously, with all the streets in town and all the places James could be looking for stranded people, why here?*

"The guy dropped me off by the gate. I saw your glove outside and . . ." He looks down again. "I got . . . worried." He holds up her glove for proof.

"I didn't even know I dropped it." Melissa fiddles with the ribbons underneath her chin and considers taking off the bonnet. *But I don't want him to think I'm embarrassed in the clothing, even if I am. I mean, who is he to have power over me?* Then she looks at him and feels everything inside her about to burst.

"By the way, you look . . ." A grin plays on James' mouth.

Melissa watches her face twist in the mirror. "Dumb, I know."

"That wasn't what I was going to say." James takes a step back from her. *Oh, great, now he's repulsed by me,* Melissa thinks and, steeling herself against the rejection, is even more determined to act normal in her flouncy dress and wounded heart.

"So." Melissa gestures widely with her arms like a game show hostess. "See anything that grabs your attention?" She blushes, hoping he didn't think she meant her. "I mean, there's a lot to choose from. . . ."

"Actually, we do have that party coming up." James rifles through a rack of soldier uniforms.

"Which party?" Instantly the stress of planning the dance floor comes rushing back. *It's so easy to get distracted by boys and their stupid cute faces,* Melissa thinks, and tries to shrug it off. *Must stay focused.*

"Gabe's bash. At the old mill—should be a great kick-off to a new year."

Melissa remembers the invite Gabe handed her—the secrecy, the illicit notions of a party that starts late and comes with an unknown guest list. "I didn't know you were going."

James frowns and stops looking at the costumes. "Oh, I didn't realize you and Gabe . . ."

Melissa shakes her head. "No, no—what do you mean? There's nothing . . ."

"Look, it's fine." James holds up his hands like he's been caught stealing something.

"There's nothing to be fine about. Seriously." Melissa walks over to the costume rack. In order to busy her hands she flicks through pile of canes and swords, and hands a dagger to James. "You could be a pirate—that's a decent costume."

James studies her. "You going as Bo Peep?"

Melissa gives him her get-real look. "No."

"What, then?"

"Don't know yet. I'll think of something." James laughs. "What? What's so funny?"

James shoves his hands into his jacket pocket and grins. "Nothing—it's just . . . Charlie? She's going as an angel and . . ."

Melissa's heart dips to her toes. *Right. Angel. Of course. Slut. I mean, angel.* "Oh, that's . . . original." Then she feels petty and mean. "Sorry—I didn't mean to insult her. It's totally not my place."

James shrugs and blows it off. "Hey, no big deal. That's what I was thinking, anyway. Why do girls always try to dress sexy or slutty for costumes?"

Melissa tries to smooth over her insult by chatting away. "I know—Cat Girl, catsuit, any excuse to wear lingerie." *I wish I didn't like him. I wish he liked me. I wish Charlie evaporated. I wish . . .* Melissa, in her scratchy dress and bonnet, turns to James. "You know, I just want to be the bigger person here. I wanted to be okay with everything but . . ."

"Um, Mesilla?" James stammers over her name, calling her *Mesilla* like he had when they first met.

Melissa rambles. "I mean, you and Charlie—so, okay, you're a thing."

"A thing?" James leans on the rack of clothing, then chooses a big umbrella from the pile of canes and sticks. It opens in his hands, producing a waterproof rainbow of colors.

"Fine—not a thing—a . . . she's your girlfriend and, by all accounts in the papers, you guys are the real deal. In love. I get it." Melissa suddenly fights the tears that spring to her eyes, desperate not to show any more than she already has.

James puts the umbrella over his shoulder as though it's really raining and comes closer to her. "You're upset. . . . Come here . . ."

"No." Melissa can't bear the thought of being close

to him, near enough to feel his breath or smell his scent of soap and chocolate. "I'm okay. Really. It was just—you're plastered all over the evening papers."

James rolls his eyes. "Those damn papers. The tabloids. Do you know they tried to break into my room at the chalet?"

"Why? What were they looking for?"

"Anything—pictures, letters, who knows." James stands looking hot and heated in his jacket, his face flushed from the cold and the conversation. "But just so you know . . . me and Charlie?"

Melissa swallows, gulping for air in her corset-topped dress. "Yeah?" She can see all around them the image of Charlie pressed against James, but at the same time she can't shake the memory of what it felt like to kiss him.

"We're not . . ." James licks his lips, twirling the umbrella so it spins. "She not my . . ." Deliberately and without pausing he walks to Melissa, pulls her to his chest, and kisses her.

The kiss is everything that Melissa wants. It's happening. Here. Now. But—"Wait. Stop." Melissa pulls back. "What about Charlie?"

James shakes his head, staring at her with intense eyes. "There never was anything. At least—not from my end of things. Maybe she wanted . . ."

"Maybe? The girl was draped on you like a coat."

James tilts Melissa's face up so he can kiss her again. "It's never been her. Only you."

They are about to kiss again when suddenly Melissa jolts backward. "Oh my god!"

"What? What, are you okay?" James looks panicked.

Smiling ear to ear, Melissa cracks up. Laughing hard, she can't believe it. She thinks about telling Dove, *So he kisses me while I'm wearing a bonnet. . . .* "Everything's better than fine. Check it out." She lets go of her grasp on James and cuts across the room to show him what caught her eye. "See? This solves the problem!"

James follows her until he's near a stack of silvery white platforms. "They look like props for a musical or something."

"Exactly. Theatrical. Like something you could use to make the chessboard in *Alice's Adventures in Wonderland*. They're perfect." Melissa's voice carries her thrill. "Can't you see it? The whole outside will be the dance floor—the huge squares layered together will form a path that winds through the pine trees, around the lake. You can put them directly on the snow and trim them with lights or keep them plain."

"And here I thought we had a moment." James grins at her. "Turns out you're all about the ball."

Melissa walks over to him, ever confident in her getup, and kisses him on the mouth. "Can we have more moments?" James nods. "Then let me make a call." She slides her hand on the smooth silvery white surface. "If there are hundreds of these, I'm golden." As she says it, she looks at James and has the feeling, even in hot pink polyester, that she just might be, anyway.

As night begins to take over the sky, snow continues to fall, piling up so high that outside the windows of the cabin, Dove can see mounds of it.

"No way you two'll make it anywhere tonight. . . . You better stay here."

Max gives a toothless smile, agreeing to the offer before Dove can say anything. The ax rests in the corner of the room, and Dove has already scouted out other implements of potential danger—the dagger on the wall, an ornamental sword displayed above the fireplace, a cabinet that could hold guns.

"Could you excuse us for a second?" Dove pulls Max by the sweater, and then when he's resistant, by the hand to the other room. His fingers on hers feel good—too good—and she drops his hand quickly.

"What's the deal?" Max looks over his shoulder to the fireside, not wanting to be rude.

"Are you kidding? We're stranded here with a complete nutcase. . . ." Dove's brow crinkles with worry. Max shakes his head, laughing. "Are you laughing at me or near me?"

"Both." Max eyes her face, his fingers twitching from the brief grasp with hers. "Didn't you notice that he—the ax man—knows my name?" Dove blushes. "On the way into town, I told you I knew the person who lived here."

"You did?" Dove reflects on the bumpy cold ride but can't remember.

"I did. My professor from Oxford, Randolph Hartman?" Max points to the man who now sits facing the fireplace. "The premier expert on Shakespearean translations and meanings—that's your creepy killer."

Dove bites her lip, feeling more than a little foolish, her skin burning as though she's forgotten the SPF. *I should be on a beach. I should be with William. I should be . . .* "So what's with all the pointy things?" Dove asks when they're back in the room with Professor Hartman.

Professor Hartman stands up, looking decidedly more professorial now that Dove knows his identity; the ratty sweater looks intellectual, his eyes wise. "My father was a keen collector. The sword on the wall there is—supposedly—from an original production of *Romeo and Juliet*."

"Greatest love story ever told," Max comments, not looking at Dove.

"I disagree." Dove puts her hands on her waist. It's the first time in ages she's had an academic thought, but it feels natural.

"Why?" Professor Hartman studies them both as though they're in a private lecture. "In what way do you think the play fails as a love story?"

"Because . . ." Suddenly Dove wonders if she has the right to an opinion. *Didn't I drop out of the game before even getting to university? What do I know—really—about great literature?*

"It's okay, go on." Professor Hartman waits for her, adding a log to the fire in the meantime.

"Because Romeo and Juliet don't actually get to be together. They have the idea of love—or maybe even the real thing—but it's never fully realized." Dove puts her hands in her pockets, thinking. "It's as though they want love and feel it, but because of the tragedy they never experience it."

Professor Hartman nods, considering her. "Interesting." He goes to the kitchen, leaving Dove and Max in silence. Soon the teapot whistles and he calls, "And in life, not plays? Is it the same thing?"

Dove sits on the floor, leaning back on Max's chair but not touching him, and wonders.

Later that night, Professor Hartman apologizes for the lack of a spare room in which Max and Dove can sleep.

Does he assume we're a couple? Dove wonders, a bit relieved not to have to sleep in an enclosed space with Max. *Out in the open of the living room; that's sure to be less of a temptation, right?*

After a bowl of stew and crunchy bread, Professor Hartman goes to bed, leaving Max and Dove with extra bedding to sleep by the fire.

"You take the extra blanket. I'll be fine." Max hands her a quilt.

Dove shakes him off. "No—I'm fine. You have it."

They stand waiting for the other to act. Dove refuses to give in, feeling that if she does take the blanket it somehow means more. *I mean, I can't have him thinking that anything's going to happen. Not even close. Surveying the scene—blizzard, snowed in, cabin, fireside, just the two of us—it seems romantic, but it won't be. Right?*

They lie down in the flickering firelight with what Dove considers an appropriate amount of space between them.

"Good night," Max says, but doesn't turn away from her.

" 'Night." Dove curls herself into a ball for warmth and looks at the embers reflecting in Max's eyes. "You know green eyes are supposed to be bad? In literature they're symbolic of an unfaithful character."

"Is that what you think of me?" Max's voice is hushed.

"No." She looks at him, wishing for a kiss and also that she didn't want him to kiss her. That feeling everything for Will were enough.

"Dove?"

"Yeah."

"Are you going to that party?" Max tucks his arms under the blankets.

"What party?" Instantly she feels left out. *After all, he's a paying guest and I'm a worker bee. He's probably been to loads of parties, with tons of famous and fun people, while I've been making beds and cooking quiches.*

"The one near the old mill—rumor has it it's the biggest of the year. Private. Costume." Max raises his eyebrows.

Dove frowns. "I don't think I'm invited. . . . So . . ."

Max shrugs, trying to be nonchalant. "Well, if you want to go, you can come with me." He sees her mouth fly open in response and clarifies. "Not as a date or anything. Just . . . a party. The spirit of the season."

Dove pushes her hair from her eyes, thinking back to when it was long enough to hide behind. "Okay. If it's the spirit of the season, it could be fun." The fire crackles, the logs burning bright red and warm.

"Can I ask you something?" Max moves just the tiniest bit closer. Dove nods. "How come—before, outside—you wouldn't take my hand?"

Dove exhales audibly, thinking. "Aside from the fact that I—"

"Have a boyfriend, yes, we all know by now . . ."

Dove waits for him to finish and then goes on. "I don't know. . . . Hand holding is, like, a thing—it's more serious than you think. It means a lot—you have to work your way up to it. I mean, out in public, not at a movie theater or in a dorm room, it's different. It's a declaration of how you feel."

"That's what you think?" Max exposes his hands, pulling them out from under the blankets.

"Yes, it is." She hopes he'll grab for her hand—right now—but he doesn't.

"Good to know." The quiet spreads between them, and the exhaustion takes over until Dove is finally asleep. She doesn't know what will happen when she wakes up, but has a sneaking suspicion that the extra blanket will be carefully—maybe lovingly—draped over her.

Mel and Dove—

I'm starting to get paranoid that you've forgotten me. Can you write or call or send a carrier pigeon? I'm sunburned, tired, and burnt out from all the beachy barbeques, boys, and beer. (They take this Jamaican beer and mix it with ginger ale and it's good, but too good. . . .) Makes me long for a solitary run down the slopes. Not sure I have what it takes to make it as an island hostess.

Wish you were here.

Harley

15

I can't believe it hasn't even been twenty-four hours. So little time and so much has happened. So much to tell Dove. If Harley were here, she'd rush out from our room just to hear about the situation, but she's not. Briefly, Melissa tries to imagine Harley in her new surroundings and wonders if she'll ever see her again.

With more than a little trepidation, Melissa heads back to the chalet, her feet dragging in the snow. Her hair is matted, her eyes slightly puffy from lack of sleep, but her heart is elated. *He likes me. He likes me,* she hears in every passing snowplow's swish. All along the roads snow is walled up high, and everywhere are resort workers starting to dig out. *Looks like we'll have our work cut out for us.* Melissa leans forward into James as they near the chalet. *Fine, so maybe it's not a black stallion, but it's close*, she thinks when James gives her a lift on his state-of-the-art snow craft. *Last night was a dream, snow filled and surreal, with a few lingering kisses, costumes and the answer to my winter gala dilemma—what more could I ask for? Oh yeah, maybe a clarification of what it all means . . .*

"I have double practices. Gotta make up for lost time." His eyes aren't visible through the helmet's tinted visor, but Melissa can feel him stare.

Not wanting to sound overly dramatic or clingy, she says, "So maybe I'll see you later?"

"Of course." He revs the engine and backs up. "And hey, Mesilla—Melissa—I'm glad you weren't stranded alone."

A grin wraps its way across her face as Melissa crunches on the snowy path toward the chalet. Standing on the balcony, her unmistakable strawberry blond hair cascading down her back, is Charlie. Trying to avoid the obvious issue of James, Melissa waves. *After all, it's better to be friendly and social than assume there's a problem.* Melissa waves again, slightly overenthused. Charlie stares back but doesn't respond. Instead, she swings her hair back and brusquely moves inside. *So much for friendly.*

"Trouble brewing?" a voice asks from behind.

Melissa swivels. "If it isn't Gabe Schroeder, meteorologist extraordinaire."

"Just call me Mister Weather."

"Okay, so you were right. I should've . . ." Melissa pauses. Should she have left town yesterday? If she had, the whole night with James wouldn't have happened. "Let's just say if skiing doesn't pan out, you could have a career as a one of those dorky yet approachable forecasters."

"Sign me up." Gabe takes the joking critique and eyes Melissa's face, her smile. His own cheeks are rosy with the brisk air, his lips red. "So I take it you made it through the storm okay?"

Melissa nods. *Better than okay.* But she doesn't say this to Gabe. Something makes her hold it back—either not trusting the night's events or maybe not trusting herself with Gabe. "What about you?"

"Oh, I got back just in time to send out the troops. After I saw you, I pretty much bolted back here, rallied everyone from the slopes and bedrooms and cars and . . . well, you know." He kicks snow from the bottom of his boots. In the background, Dove's easy stride is visible, her bright blond hair blending in with the snow.

Melissa waves to Dove. "What do you mean? What troops?"

"Oh, we all got sent out last night—to check on people." Melissa is sure a blush can be seen on her cheeks but she tries to fight it. *James found me. He checked up on me.* Gabe clears his throat, the nervous kind of noise not the true cough. "Actually, it's kind of funny. I was going to come find you. . . ."

Melissa feels her stomach tighten. "Me? Wait—where?"

"In town. After I went back in for a last patrol, I thought I saw your glove outside this old factory place. . . . But when I looked again, it was gone."

So Gabe found my dropped glove first, not James. Melissa holds up both hands so she can show Gabe her wool-covered fingers. "Got 'em both right here." *Why would James say he'd found it? And does it matter? He came to see me, right?* "Anyway, thanks for thinking of me."

Gabe shrugs and smiles. "No biggie—as long as you're all right."

"She looks fine to me," Dove says, overhearing the conversation as she approaches. She and Melissa lock eyes, conveying without words the need to tell their stories—quickly, before they burst. *She looks better than fine,* Dove thinks, biting her lip and thinking simultaneously about the fireside night, the plane ticket in her room that may or may not be used, and how on earth she'll make twelve hundred mincemeat pies and dust them with confectionary sugar in time for Matron's private tea. *I mean, Matron could have given me warning, but no—she chose to announce this tea to me now, on my way back from a snowstorm. Now the deluge of baking must ensue.* Dove looks at the chalet with a mixture of relief and contempt.

"We have to go. . . . Sorry." Melissa looks at Gabe and adds, "Thanks for thinking of me yesterday, though."

Dove raises her eyebrows at this but doesn't comment.

"Don't let me keep you from all your duties. But remember—tomorrow night, right?" Gabe's wink is over-the-top obvious and Melissa laughs.

"Yeah, I think I remember. P-A-R-T-Y. I'll be there with bells on." She thinks about what costume she could possibly wear, wonders if the secret party will be as cool as everyone says or if it'll end like most parties, with sticky-sweet drinks, an emptying crowd, and another night gone by. "Well, maybe not bells, but . . ."

"Come on." Dove yanks her by the jacket. "You have some serious hosting to do and I have only about a million pies to make for Matron and a billion crepes to cook for the guests to make up for lost time. . . ."

"Isn't it so weird to have such a crazy night and come back here to find it's all the same?" Melissa grabs a glass of orange juice before her next hosting gig.

Dove nods. "I know, it's like going back to school after summer when you know you've changed—or you think you have. And then you get to school and it's all the same old, same old." She adds butter to the industrial-sized mixer in front of her and wipes her hands on her apron. "Not that I'd know about back-to-school these days."

"What's that supposed to mean?" Melissa finishes the juice and washes her glass so Charlie won't have to do it later, rinsing the few plates in the sink also. *Maybe if I tiptoe around her, Charlie won't mind that I won the tug-of-war over James.*

Shrugging, Dove switches the mixer on, watching the butter and sugar blend together in a swirl of creamy yellow. "I don't know. . . . It's just—last night, talking about Shakespeare and thinking about all the literature I know about and the plays and books I *don't* know about . . ."

Melissa flicks the mixer off so she can hear Dove better. "You miss school!" Melissa flings water onto Dove's face.

"Hey!" Dove wipes the spray off her cheeks, laughing.

"Yeah, wake up, Dove. Miss Lily de Whatever Title Society Girl . . . you want to go back to school, don't you?"

Dove shakes her head, adding flour and a pinch of cinnamon to the mixing bowl. "I never said that."

"Oh, okay."

"Anyway, enough about me. What are you going to do about—" Dove's question is cut off by the abrupt appearance of Charlie in the doorway.

"What's she going to do about what?" Charlie's

hands perch on her hips, and she eyes Dove and Melissa with suspicion.

Dove goes back to cooking. "Hi, Charlie. I was just asking . . ."

"She wanted to know if I'd sorted out the next big activity," Melissa says, covering for Dove, who was clearly about to address the Charlie-James conundrum.

"And have you?" Charlie cocks her head to one side, her body elegant in black leggings and an oversized cashmere sweater.

Only she would wear cashmere to clean toilets. Melissa fights the urge to ask Charlie what she did during the storm, knowing that if the question were turned back, there'd be no way of avoiding the kiss with James. Just thinking about his lips on hers makes Melissa stammer. "Um, yeah. Actually, um, everything's fine." She checks her watch more as a gesture than because she really needs to know the time. "An hour and I'll be directing the ice painting out on the pond."

"Painting?" Charlie's voice patronizes her almost as much as the look she gives. "Isn't that a bit childish?"

Now it's Dove's turn to spring into defensive mode. "Ice painting is a Trois tradition. For over one hundred years skiers and guests have gathered on the pond with paints. . . ."

"In this case, ecologically sound food coloring," Melissa adds. "It's fun. Really."

Charlie sighs. "Suit yourself."

Dove and Melissa exchange a look. Melissa takes a deep breath and voices what they're both thinking. "Charlie?" Charlie responds with only a look of boredom. "When did you become so . . ." Melissa stops herself.

Dove fills in. "Such a bitch?"

Charlie hardly reacts. "Oh, you mean because I was so nice last week?" She licks her lips and remains placid. "Personalities are just things to change as you need to."

"So you're a chameleon of niceness to nastiness?" Dove asks, her face disbelieving.

Charlie shrugs. "Works back home. It's every person for themselves—and if there's fallout along the way, so be it."

"That's a pretty grim way of looking at it," Melissa says.

Charlie looks exasperated. "You can both keep up the pretense of closeness, but underneath, everyone's just in it for themselves."

Fed up with her roommate's attitude, Dove shakes her head. "Don't you have some bathrooms to mop or beds to make?" Dove manages to ask this in a way that isn't obviously insulting, but cutting nonetheless.

"What I do and don't do is my concern. Isn't it?" She walks over to the mixing bowl, sticks a finger into Dove's batter and tries it. "Not bad. Could use a bit more sugar, though."

I could say the same thing about you, both Melissa and Dove think at the same time. Dove flinches—it's her biggest pet peeve to have people sample things before they're ready. *Maybe I'm like that, too,* she thinks. *I can't act until I'm well and truly ready. Like with Max. Or school. Or . . . William.* She imagines the plane ticket to the West Indies waiting for her downstairs. Just a couple of days and the flight will board.

"I have to get back to my reading," Charlie says, and in a last flashy attempt to show who's boss, unfurls the newspaper from under her arm to reveal yet another snapshot of her with James.

"Isn't that yesterday's paper?" Melissa asks, her heart beating hard.

Charlie gives her a stare worthy of its own storm warnings. "No. This is today's." Charlie smiles, showing her camera-worthy teeth. "And P.S., just so you know, I have some big news to tell." She pauses for dramatic effect. "But not yet." She studies the paper. Front and center is a different photo of James kissing Charlie's cheek. It's this image that Charlie leaves Melissa with before clomping down the stairs.

"Don't worry about it—I'm sure it means nothing," Dove says, and begins searching for the vanilla extract.

"I don't know what to think anymore. All I know is that I have to be on the ice and ready to go in forty minutes."

16

All across the expanse of frozen water, myriad colors make the pond look like an outdoor work of art.

Melissa listens to comments from onlookers.

"This is amazing!"

"How unusual!"

"The prizes this year are better than ever. . . ."

Various languages blend with the cold air, as the colors spread across the pond. Bottles of different-hued food coloring are available on tables by the ice edge: blue, magenta, yellow, green, and a bunch of metallics—the food coloring to which Melissa added an organic biodegradable silver, gold, or copper. Guests help themselves to squeeze bottles and then set to work making pictures or designs. Off to one side, kids have a field day, squirting themselves as much as the ice. On the other side, the more professional-looking artists work in careful drips and dots, creating recognizable monuments, familiar faces, or flowers.

Melissa walks carefully on the ice, promising herself she won't fall. Not again. *The last thing I need for Gabe's party and the ball is to be laid up in a cast or limping. Yeah, that'd be a sexy costume. Not that James likes those clichéd costumes. And not that I'm going to dress for him, but still . . .*

"Hello? Miss Forsythe?"

"What? Sorry." Melissa snaps to attention as Matron gives her a disapproving look.

"Ten minutes and then we'll do the judging." Matron looks at the smiles, the general pleasure among the crowds of people painting and watching, and has to give a nod to Melissa. "Even though you seem as though you're off on another planet, I must commend you on a job well done." She watches a woman squirt a bottle of blue food coloring up into the air so that when it hits the ice it freezes in a display similar to fireworks.

"Thanks. I don't feel like I did all that much. I mean it's just some paint and . . ."

Matron puts her hand on Melissa's shoulder. "Will you wake up and smell reality? We've had tons of hosts here. Hundreds. Boys with backgrounds that suited them toward military school or brilliant banking. Girls whose beauty kept them going through anything or who did a fine enough job but who didn't come by any of the organizing naturally."

"And I do?" Melissa smiles, her eyes almost afraid of looking right at Matron.

"You might be slightly dreamy . . ." Matron watches Melissa notice Charlie across the pond. "Or slightly socially inclined. But . . . you are very organized and very enthusiastic and personable."

Melissa shrugs, trying to be humble. "I just set up all the bottles on Changeover Day. I mean, with the schedule planned out, and using food coloring, not paint, I just made a box of each shade and labeled them and . . ."

Matron puts her finger to her lips. "The best hosts never ruin the magic." Matron takes a bottle of red and squeezes it into a dribbly heart. "Make it look easy, and know in your heart it's not."

Melissa takes in the praise and the works of ice art while trying to avoid Charlie, who seems eager to find her. As Charlie heads for the refreshment stand, Melissa slinks along the edge of the ice, eyeing the enormous rendering of the Eiffel Tower, a full waterway with gondola in Venice, and a bouquet of sunflowers as a homage to van Gogh. Then, right when she's about to alert Matron to the ice painting worthy of the biggest prize (in this case, use of the resort's private jet to anywhere in the world for two), Melissa stops in her tracks.

"Oh my god."

There, on the ice, among the smiley faces drawn in yellow, the pretty but not spectacular flowers and abstract artwork, is—

"Holy crap." Dove bounds onto the ice, looking like a fairy complete with white-dusted hair and eyelashes. Only her dusting is with flour, not sparkles.

"I know, right?" Melissa stands agog at the site in front of her. In one-dimensional form is a perfect replica of the world-famous Mona Lisa painting. "It's so real."

"I know." Dove nods. "I've been to the Louvre countless times and this is almost better than the original. . . . At least this one's big enough to get a good look at."

Melissa kneels down to touch the frozen paint, forgetting it came from a squeeze bottle, forgetting it's food coloring she herself had dumped into the plastic containers, forgetting everything except the picture. "It's not my imagination, though, right? I mean it's—"

"Oh, it's completely not your imagination. Everyone—anyone could tell that this isn't just the *Mona Lisa.* It's a portrait of you."

"Look—there's no signature, though." Melissa traces her own facial features with a gloved hand, wondering who might have taken the time to do this and why. "All the other ones have unmistakable names underneath."

"Well, no one wants to miss out on the prizes, I guess."

Melissa swivels on her knees to check out the scene. Matron makes her rounds, jotting notes about the finalists for the prizes. The guests begin to head for the refreshment stand, warming themselves on oversized mugs of hot chocolate or spiked eggnog. "What should I do? I can't very well nominate this for a prize. Not unless I want to win the Most Conceited award."

"No. You can't nominate this for top place," Dove says.

"But I can." Matron stands with a smug grin, looking down at Melissa. "There aren't any rules governing what art is acceptable, nor which subjects." She shakes her head, remembering. "Considering the filth we got a few years back, just be glad the artist chose *Mona Lisa* and not a centerfold of some kind . . ."

Melissa laughs hearing Matron say the word *centerfold*.

Dove wipes some flour from her cheeks. "I have to run if I'm going to finish dusting these pies."

Matron turns to her. "I trust you're ready for the tea?"

Dove nods. "Just about. Everything's cooling in the kitchen. I'll transport it to the Oak Library shortly."

"Are you coming to the prize ceremony?" Matron asks Melissa.

Still on the ice, Melissa touches the picture one more time, feeling that whoever painted it somehow captured an element of her she hardly knew she had, but one that immediately announced itself as hers. It's like she—the girl in this painting—knows something. About life. About love. And she's so sure of it—that's why she's smiling. She's got something to look forward to that's different. Off the path and into life.

Melissa stands up, a smile twin to the one on the Faux Lisa gracing her mouth. "Don't I have to be there to hand out the prizes?"

Matron shakes her head. "No. I'll be there and can certainly manage. Perhaps you have tidying up to do before . . ."

Melissa is a mere mouthful away from spewing *the party* to Matron when she realizes her supervisor means the ball. "Right. Tomorrow. The big event."

"So many years of wonderful galas. Let's hope the Winter Wonderland lives up to the expectations. That it surpasses them."

Melissa nods, the stress of all the planning coming back to her. She leaves the skating pond and all the colors, the tribute to herself, and the anonymity of the artist, so she can rush back to the chalet.

17

Set back from the main resort area toward the heavily wooded land where the original resort stood, Dove feels a bit of anxiety mingling with the cozy atmosphere of the Oak Library. *Hard to believe this building was once the main building of the whole resort, with just tiny cabins scattered into the mountainside. I wish it were like that still. No ritz, no glamour, no outpouring of wealth and class. Just nature and skiing. And maybe love.* Dove readies the last tray of mince pies, dusting their tops with sugar in the shape of a holly leaf.

Amid the quiet chatter about ski conditions and the upcoming New Year, Dove spots Professor Randolph

Hartman taking not one but two of her mince pies. When he realizes he's been caught, he offers a loud guffaw.

"Wasn't it Wittgenstein who favored excess of pastries?" he asks, and joins Dove by her station. She ladles eggnog and hot buttered rum into clear glass mugs, topping each one with a dollop of freshly made whipped cream.

She shoots him a doubtful glance. "I'm not so sure about that."

"But you are sure about some things, aren't you?" He bites into a pie and makes noises of delight. "These are wonderful. I have you to thank for them, do I?"

Dove nods. "My nanny's old recipe." She blushes, wondering if that sounds silly.

"Looks as though you're in no need of a nanny these days." Randolph finishes the first pie and sips from his mug.

"Oh, I wouldn't be so sure of that." Dove busies herself with folding cocktail napkins and handing a drink to a tweed-clothed invitee. "Sometimes I think I could still use someone to tell me where to go and what to do. . . ." She laughs, trying to make light of what she said.

"Maybe that's not such a bad idea." Professor Hartman looks at her over the rims of his glasses, causing his eyes to look small and kind. He puts down his pie and rests his drink on the table, searching his pockets for something. "Here."

"What's this?" Dove takes the card he hands her and looks at the number on it.

"It's my office number." He resumes eating the pie and then speaks with his mouth full. "Last night . . ."

Dove makes a face. "Ugh. Last night . . ." *It seems like ages ago. Talking about books. Lying there with Max. Wanting him to . . .*

"Maxwell spent the better part of his first term at Oxford in tutorials with me. Granted, I assign on average one thousand pages of reading a week and a minimum of thirty written pages to be read aloud in the sanctuary that I call my office."

Dove listens, wondering why he's telling her this, but nods. "Max is a good student."

"He is. Quite good. From what he says—from what he's said all term—and from discussing things with you last night . . . well, it seems as though you're a better student. Or a more critical thinker."

"Oh, I'm critical all right." Dove instantly recalls arguments with her parents about staying at Les Trois, about being cut off from the family finances, how her mother and father accused her of being too critical of the place that she came from.

As if reading her mind, Professor Hartman says, "We're all products, at least in some way, of where we're brought up. Or maybe we're not and one could argue that in a paper. One might argue that trying to actively escape the chains of upbringing could only plunge us deeper into denial."

Dove reaches for a mug of rum and drinks some, despite knowing it's against the rules. "So you're saying . . ."

"I'm saying that you can fight it all you like, but it's my opinion—and Max's, I might add—that you think about rejoining the academic ranks and go to university."

Dove swallows. The liquor burns her throat, and the idea put forth by the axman-turned-professor seems just as sharp. A painful departure from the self-driven life she's leading now to papers, lectures, and home turf. "I don't know." First she lets her thoughts run away, with her mouth following closely behind. "There are plans I've made, you know? Beaches, boys—it probably sounds stupid to you. But it's my life, and I'm living it even if it isn't . . ." She stops. What isn't it? Easy? Fun? Exciting? Good for the long run? *What, exactly, was my plan after this season, anyway?* Blushing at her lack of forethought, Dove's manners come back to her and she does what her mother always taught her to in situations that could be awkward. She glosses over and doesn't deal. "You're very kind to suggest I've somehow retained the intellectual capacity to go . . . or that they'd even have me after I never enrolled. I do appreciate your point of view."

Professor Hartman watches her with a mix of amusement and frustration. "I understand." He wipes his mouth on the napkin and drains his drink. "Please do get in touch should you ever feel like responding in a real way to what I've said."

He shakes her hand and leaves her to ladle eggnog and contemplate what she would have said if she'd been telling the truth.

"So what's her big surprise, anyway?" Just out of the shower, Melissa rummages in her bureau for anything that could pass as a costume. "You realize we have to leave in five minutes and I have nothing to wear, haven't eaten all day practically, and have the ball to contend with tomorrow starting at the crack of dawn."

"And you realize that most of your nerves aren't due to any of those issues but have merely to do with seeing a certain James again. . . ." Dove slides into an entirely silver bodysuit. "What do you think?"

Melissa raises her eyebrows, checking out the full view. "Um, I think it doesn't leave much to the imagination."

"I'm meant to be a snowflake." Dove plays with her white blond hair, spiking it with hair wax. She rims her mouth with iridescent lipstick, completing her look.

"Great. You look like a stunning, if a tad slutty, snowflake, and I'm a big wad of nothing." Melissa holds up a scarf and large hoop earrings. "Whenever I didn't know what to wear for Halloween, I always went as a pirate."

"All the scarves, layers, and jewelry you could want . . . not to mention eyeliner." Dove laughs. "Come on, just hurry and find something so we can get there."

A knocking at the back door surprises both of them. "You think it's Charlie?"

"What does she want? To rub her mysterious secret in our faces again?" Melissa tromps over to the door, ready to inform Charlie that neither she nor Dove cares to hear about her big announcement. But at the back door is Matron, with a worried look on her face.

"Are you okay?" Melissa asks. She tries to ascertain what the issue at hand is so that Matron won't come in and see Dove in costume. Off-resort parties would not be tolerated. Melissa taps her foot, not wanting to be late.

"I've just had a thought." Matron furrows her brow. "You've solved the issue with the flooring for the ball, but what about the ice?"

"Sorry?" Melissa thinks about ice—for drinks? For sculptures? For . . . "Oh, you want the ice cleaned?"

Matron looks apologetic—or as apologetic as she gets late at night. "I know it's a bit last-minute to spring on you, but I've had a look at the pond in the moonlight and it's just too much. Too much muddled colors and graffiti. The rather rowdy skiers took over after we left and, well, you can imagine the state they've left it in."

Melissa nods, the sinking feeling of missing the party

to end all parties creeping into her thoughts. "And you want me to do this now?"

"There's a hose and sprayer all hooked up for you. Shouldn't take but a few minutes."

Two hours later, Melissa stands with her teeth chattering, spraying the last quarter of the pond. *A few minutes, my ass. This is taking forever. By now Dove's probably in lip lock with Max, and Charlie's gathering a crowd for her major attention-grabbing statement. And James? Will he wait for me? Understand why I'm not there? Or be dancing with someone else?*

Melissa's hand grips the nozzle, spraying a steady stream of water that freezes almost immediately after hitting the ice. The layer of new ice covers over the colors, muting them into submission.

When she gets to the Mona Lisa portrait, Melissa can't bring herself to cover it. *Fine. Let Matron have a fit. It's a job mostly well done. But the Mona Melissa is too nice to cover up. And it's the first time someone ever did anything like that for me.* She checks her watch. *If I leave from here, I can just about make the party.*

Melissa follows the directions given to her, in French, by a farmer out with his dogs, and wonders if she misheard him. *The cold place? Maybe even he knows it's a cool party. But not cold.* She drives the van slowly, hoping not to miss the turn that will lead her to where the lights are. Even from where she is, she can make out a source of light—spotlights in blue. She rolls down the window, thinking she can hear music, and sure enough, the steady thump of bass swooshes over the fields and hills, beckoning her closer.

The van pauses on a bridge and Melissa has to use the windshield wipers to clear the steam from the front window. *What the . . . Oh. Cold. Not cool. But cool, too.* Towering in front of her, past the parked cars, the wide lights flanking the bridge, are the guests decked out in costumes that make Melissa bemoan her own red snowpants and jacket. But farther on is a building made entirely of ice.

So much for dressing in slips and lingerie, Melissa thinks as she parks and heads toward the entrance. Women in slim-fitting angel outfits shiver, while others in princess gear and Catwoman suits rub their hands on their arms for warmth.

"Welcome to the ice palace!" A bouncer stands checking invites at the cavernous doorway. Melissa flashes hers and pauses, agape at the sheer beauty of the building.

A ski team member stands spewing information for anyone to hear. "Four stories, thirty-five rooms, two bars, and all made of fresh water from the Le Monde River. Pretty amazing, huh?"

Melissa nods, entranced. Only the feeling of being costumeless and clunky in her red snowsuit makes her frown. *Why am I not one of those girls?* She eyes the nearest angel-slash-lingerie model and feels even bulkier. Just as she's having the momentary lack of confidence, Charlie appears.

"Hey, nice costume, Melissa." Charlie's sarcasm drips from her faux smile. Dressed as an elf, if elves were inherently gorgeous, Charlie's red tights, knee-high black boots, and felt minidress only make Melissa more self-conscious. *So she's not an angel—how fitting,* Melissa thinks. Before Melissa can react with a comeback, Charlie waves to someone up on the ice balcony above them.

Melissa looks up. *James. Of course.* James looks down, waves at them both and makes a move toward the curved ice stairs.

"Looks like we have company," Melissa says.

"Correction: *I* have company. You just have a big red suit."

The only saving grace is the fact that she's cold. Melissa watches Charlie rub her hands together, bouncing slightly in her boots. Along the wall are massive black coats for the taking. Charlie looks longingly at the puffy jackets but doesn't reach for one. In a bin near the coats are castoff accessories—glittery headbands, swords, an umbrella, and a few angel wings.

"It's just a coat—it won't bite you," Melissa says, wishing the image of Charlie and James weren't quite so vivid in her mind. Big news, she has big news. It could be anything, right? Not necessarily about her and—

"Hey! Glad you could make it!" James leans in to greet Melissa.

He's going to kiss me—right here, in front of everyone, in front of his tabloid love. She waits, tilting her head just a little. But James only kisses her cheek, then checks out her outfit. "And what is this, exactly?"

Charlie butts in. "She's not anything. She's just in snow gear."

I'm not anything. That can't be true, though. Melissa feels a surge of anger and frustration somehow morph into calm. "Oh, I'm something all right. First of all, I'm warm." Melissa points to Charlie's blue lips, her shivers. "You'd think all the females in this place had something to prove. . . ."

James laughs, turning conspiratorially toward Melissa. "Remember? What'd I tell you about dressing up and dressing in not enough clothing?"

Melissa dashes to the bin of extra accessories and flings through a few before grabbing a red headband with devil horns. She puts it on her own head of dark ringlets.

"Oh, now what are you supposed to be?" Charlie rolls her eyes, sidling up to James. "I'm Santa's helper. . . . But I can help you, too." She slings her arm around him just like in the paparazzi pictures. Melissa waits for James to mind, but he doesn't.

Melissa displays her red pants, red jacket, and red horns. *James doesn't go for slutty costumes, but does he go for girls in red-padded suits?* "I'm a daredevil." Melissa thinks about all the things she can do for dares.

From behind her, Gabe gives a hug. "Great costume, Melissa. Plus, you'll be warm enough." He gestures to the long ice bar. "Now, who's up for getting a cold drink?"

Tucked into a corner booth carved out of ice, Dove sips her icy drink and leans further into Max than she planned. *It's cold, that's all. And he's warm. And he's lovely.*

"So, what do you make of this place?" Gabe asks with Melissa nearby.

"Do you have to ask?" Dove smiles; having changed her outfit, she's decked out in head-to-toe silver. She pats her puffy jacket. "I'm just glad I came as tinsel. Otherwise, I'd be frostbitten by now."

Gabe nods. "We have a first-aid truck out back for just that reason." He shakes his head. "Lots of fallen angels."

Max sighs, staring at Dove, his cheeks ruddy. "Well, it's getting late. I'm gonna head out."

Dove looks surprised. *I thought he'd be here with me. Or stay with me until . . . Maybe that's the problem. I think he'll just wait for me but he won't. He has a life and I . . .*

"Well, as the party's official daredevil, I hereby command you to . . ." Melissa falters. "To give a kiss to one deserving woman before you go."

Crowds from the bar swell onto the ice floor, the music pounding, as Max stands there. "Who says I have to accept your dare?"

Melissa laughs, tipsy, and knowing she'll pay for it tomorrow when she has to organize the entire ball. "I say. I am, after all, THE DAREDEVIL."

Max looks at Dove for a long time, giving her reason to suddenly feel like jumping up and hanging on him like real tinsel. *I like him. That's the plain and simple truth.* "Are you going to come home?" Max asks her. She looks at him, confused. "To England. Go to Oxford, like you're supposed to?"

Dove feels kicked. "Oh, that's what this is about? My attending the fine institution? Or is it really about you deciding what's best for me?"

Max shakes his head. "I'll take that as a no, then." Then he turns to Melissa. "I hate dares, but just this once I'll humor you." He grabs the nearest girl from the bar, swings her around so she faces him, and plants a long kiss on her mouth. Dove watches this with her heart racing, her mind doing the same.

The girl stands up from the kiss and smiles. "Well, hello, Max. Long time no see."

Claire? My evil old friend? This just couldn't get any worse. Dove sips her drink, shoots Melissa a mean look, and hunkers down on the ice bench, feeling very cold.

The light on the ice palace competes with the light pushing its way into the morning sky.

"I should go," Melissa announces to the stragglers. *So much for the perfect night—I pissed off the best friend I have here, never even danced with James, and didn't manage to use my daredevil powers for anything good.* In the driveway, she can see Charlie getting into one of the hotel vans. *She never made her big announcement—probably it never even existed.*

"Well, thanks for coming." Gabe hugs her. "If anyone can pull off an impromptu costume, it's you."

Melissa blushes, holding the red headband in her hand. "How do you know this wasn't the product of weeks of planning?" She laughs.

Gabe's eyes sparkle as he takes the headband from her and puts it, crooked, on his own head. "So, does this thing give me special powers, too?"

Melissa shrugs. "Why? What were you hoping? To fly somewhere exotic?"

Gabe negs that idea. "Too much ski practice. Besides, I don't need wings to fly."

"Besides sounding like a cheesy lyric, what does that mean?"

Gabe clears his throat, about to explain. "I wouldn't need wings because I . . ."

"Hey, I thought I missed you." James strides over to them. He puts his arm around Melissa's shoulders. Melissa can't help but feel tingles, those magnetic vibes.

If only I didn't have to get back to the chalet and get ready for the big day and night . . . "Where were you, anyway? I was in the bar, and even ventured to the ice caves, but I didn't see you."

Gabe tugs at his bright blond curls, his emotions hidden as he waits for James to answer. "It was so crowded, you know? I looked for you, but to no avail." James squeezes her before letting go. "But tonight?"

Gabe steps in. "The big thing, right? All your hard work finally coming to fruition?"

Melissa nods, the reality of it setting in. "Yeah. The Winter Wonderland Ball. Oh my god, I so have to go." She laughs. "Gabe, it's been better than cool—it's been cold." Looking at him now, she can't help but remember that night on the mountaintop with him, back when they were more than friends. Back before everything got mixed up. James clears his throat, breaking her reverie and making Melissa refocus on him. *After all, James is everything anyone could want.*

"So I'll see you tonight, then?" Gabe raises his eyebrows. The tension is palpable between all three.

"I'll be there," Melissa says, and looks to James.

"I'll be there, too." James fiddles with his zipper and furrows his brow. "By the way, how'd the ice painting go?"

Melissa turns back. "It rocked. People had fun and there was this . . ." She starts to explain the Mona Lisa, but then suddenly wonders—*Did James paint it? Is that why he's been shy tonight?* Maybe the painting is a declaration of more than just good art skills. "It was fun."

Gabe waves as she walks off. "Glad to hear it." James concurs. "See you."

See you, Melissa thinks, wondering who really painted the picture, what Charlie's announcement is, why James was notably absent after their lip lock during the blizzard, and what exactly Gabe might have dared if there'd been more time. *See you both. Tonight.*

URGENT FAX:
To: Lily de Rothschild and Melissa Forsythe (the Tops Chalet)

Dove—surprised by the use of your REAL name? Who knew you had such secrets? Wish you'd had the faith in me to confide. . . . Seems this island of Nevis is popular with your lot—British society people, that is. I've been meaning to track down William, but I haven't—yet.

Melissa—Some big-time young chef from your Aussie nation has landed here for a celebrity restaurant launch. Met him the other night at a Fizz Party (all champagne, all on the cliffs).

The urgent notice is to get you to write back. I want news from the chalet! What happened with the ski boys? Not that I've been thinking too much about them . . . I just might have my own romantic designs here.

Love and bubbles, Harley

18

"When it comes to life, my philosophy is, whatever is meant to be will happen." Charlie says the words as though she's the first person to ever utter them. "You'll see when I make my big announcement."

"I'm not alone in thinking this big announcement of yours is a load of crap, you know." Dove nudges by Charlie, desperate to shower.

"I would have made it last night if it hadn't been so damn cold in that place. Who makes buildings out of ice?"

Dove doesn't want to get into a battle. She just wants to get clean. "Excuse me. I have eggs in my hair and frosting on my face. Can I get in here, please?"

"I'm deep conditioning," Charlie says, blocking the shower stall.

"Why? So you look good for the piles of wood chips that need to be vacuumed upstairs. You have to help clean, Charlie. I'm up to my neck in pastries and Melissa is busy doing—" Dove sighs. *I've had enough of her attitude.*

"Melissa's busy doing nothing, as far as I can see, except throwing herself at a certain skier who could care less."

Dove opens her mouth to refute the claim but then decides that saying nothing is more powerful a statement.

Charlie pivots, staring into the mirror at her own reflection while talking at Dove. "As I was saying, I believe that what's meant to be, happens. And this . . ." She points to her well-conditioned locks and her frame in general. "This is what's meant to be."

"I have no idea what you're talking about. All I know is that I need to get in there." *Before I schlep thousands of pastry icicles down to the lake. Before I help Melissa with whatever else needs doing before the grand finale to holiday week. Before I actually deal with the fact that Max kissed Claire. Before I pack my bags and head to Nevis—tomorrow.*

Charlie jumps into the shower, turning the water on so hot the steam rises instantly and fogs the mirror. Dove watches as her own reflection clouds, and hoists herself up on the counter to wait her turn. *The past days are a blur of made-to-order omelets, hand-rolled biscuits, bending over backward to cook any- and everything, and all for tips. Add in a whole lot of confusion and that's where I am. How good it'll feel to know I'm headed for the land of relaxation.*

"Just so you know," Dove says, rummaging through the drawers for any of her toiletries, lest she forget to pack them, "I don't subscribe to that point of view. I think that you make your own destiny." *And I, for one, intend to make mine.*

"What's that expression about a chicken with no head?" one of the other Chalet Girls says under her breath to Melissa.

"Tell me about it." Melissa tracks Matron's movements with her eyes, swiveling this way and that, racing here and there while seeming to accomplish nothing but flustering those around her.

"We have so much to accomplish. Simply too much. You, over there, bring me the chargers. We need those on the tables."

Melissa chews on the inside of her cheek until it hurts, then approaches Matron. "Um, Matron?"

"What now? Did you sort out the dessert issues? Where are the icicles? I thought you said those were taken care of." Matron flings her arms around, gesturing first to the empty tables that need moving and then to the outside, where extra lights are being fitted into the trees.

Melissa takes a breath, pretending she's back in Australia, surfing or at least chilling out rather than here in Stressville. "Matron . . . the thing is that we can't put the chargers out until five or so or they'll get too cold. The tables do need to be moved, but not until the lights are all strung up. And yes, I have the icicle pastries. They're on their way."

At least they better be. Dove might still be annoyed that I put Max up to the kiss, but as far as I'm concerned, it's better to know things than to not. So he kissed Claire. Deal with it and move on. Melissa then feels guilty for thinking this and decides to tell Dove exactly what she feels when she sees her.

A few minutes later, Dove appears out of breath and carrying a load of the icicles boxed in oversized Tupperware. "Some help would be good here."

"Don't bite my head off," Melissa says, taking the box from Dove. She sets it down and goes outside to a dolly where many more boxes are stacked. "I've been working all day." She takes note of Dove's wet hair. "Not all of us had the time to shower."

"Look," Dove snipes at her, "don't begrudge me that. If you reeked of eggs and syrup you'd have showered, too." She pauses. "Unless, of course, you were dared not to."

Melissa makes a sarcastic face and balances one of the boxes on her hip while deciding what to say. "You know what? I dared him. But I didn't make him slobber all over Claire."

"He didn't slobber." Dove's small features seem dwarfed in her down coat, her lips chapped. *So Claire won our age-old battle. She likes him and clearly he likes her back. His loss.*

"So now you're defending him? Which is it, Dove—do you despise him or desire him?" Melissa fights the urge to pry off the lid of the box to check and see how the pastries turned out. After all, it's her job on the line with the whole event.

"Why'd you even do it? If you hadn't dared him, maybe he'd have . . ."

"What—kissed you good night? And then where would you be? On a plane to Nevis? I seriously doubt it. You'd ditch William and all your plans."

Dove sighs and then groans. "Ughhh! What are we doing? Clawing at each other just because we can?" She sits on the stone steps and motions for Melissa to join her.

"Look." Dove lifts the lid of one of the boxes, displaying the symmetrical pastries inside. Some are white, some silver, and some have the faintest glow of pink or blue underneath a gloss of white. Each is strung by a bit of silver ribbon. "Edible icicles."

Melissa tilts her head, admiring. "Oh, Dove, they're incredible. You worked so hard. . . ." She puts her hand on Dove's back. The pale palette of pastries holds her gaze until Melissa sighs. "I'm sorry for starting the dare debacle."

"And I'm sorry for being a bitch about it. It's not you. It's my own issues." Dove ruffles her hair with both hands, causing it to go every which way like a newborn chick. "I just wanted . . ." She lowers her voice. "Him to kiss me. To make a move."

"To decide, once and for all, how it's going to be." Melissa asks with her eyes if she can try an icicle.

"Have this one—it's a little lopsided." Dove breaks it into two pieces and they munch on it while contemplating. "You're right. I just felt like maybe if he kissed me, then it meant something. Like holding hands." She thinks back to their hand-holding conversation in the cabin. "But maybe that's my problem. He's deciding everything—what I should do, where I should go, if we should get together."

"Sounds like you've thought about this."

"I have thought about it. This place . . ." Dove cranes her neck so she can see the trails dotted with skiers, the hotel with its helipad—filled now with people arriving just for the big event—and the place where she vacationed as a kid, where she met William. "I have to go. If I stay here just to wait it out, I'll regret it. And if I wind up at

Oxford or coming back here—who knows. Either way, at least I'll have followed through with everything."

"Besides, you just want to know what Harley's been up to." Melissa cracks up. "Harley, our little wild child gone tropical."

"I shudder to think." Dove stands up. Behind the Main House, a crowd of photographers is gathering, their flashes illuminating the already bright daylight. "Check it out—must be the princes, the film stars and the hangers-on."

"I've had enough of that crew," Melissa says. She squints, thinking she can make out Charlie's head of hair among the crowd.

Dove points to the icicles. "I'll finish taking these in. Should give you a few minutes to start on another project while I distract Matron."

"Thanks." Over by the parking lot, Melissa sees a delivery truck pull up. "The squares—my dance floor. They're here!" Melissa gives an excited little jump and marches off, turning only once to say, "I think we might actually do this. We just might pull it off!"

Dear Melissa and Dove,

Left a phone message for you both but still haven't heard anything back. I'm taking this to mean that you're annoyed at me. Well, fine. But just so you know, I have no regrets leaving Les Trois. Well, almost none.

If you're ever sick of the cold and snow and want to look me up . . . well, good luck. I seem to be living a nomadic existence here. Things with the host family aren't really working out, so now I'm jobless and penniless. But tan . . . and maybe in love. But that's not a story for a postcard.

Hope you get over whatever's bugging you and GET IN TOUCH. Gotta run—I'm temping at the front of the house (that's restaurant speak for hostessing) for that Aussie chef I told you about (can you say icon *and* about to have his own cooking-slash-talk show?*). The restaurant is all drapery and airy sheets billowing from tents—very* Casablanca *(at least, that's what Chef says—I've never seen that movie).*

Here's looking at you, kids.

—Harley

19

Okay—the generator's set just in case there's some sort of electrical failure; the floor tiles are all in place; the lights are bright but not too; the food is plated onto sterling chargers, set into chafing dishes, and being passed around by butlers; and the crew has fair warning about who's royalty and who's famous, who expects to dance with whom, and . . .

"And what about you?" Matron interrupts Melissa's thoughts.

"What about me?" Melissa scans the darkened air for any signs of trouble, a breaking glass, anyone falling in the snow, anyone on the ice sliding just a bit too much.

"Aren't you going to take pause?" Matron's outfit betrays the occasion. Instead of anything formal, she blends into the background in her plain gray wool skirt and quilted vest.

"I hadn't really considered that. I mean, I've been so frazzled trying to—"

"Exactly my point. You've had an unbelievable week. Take a minute to appreciate your efforts." She pats Melissa lightly on the back and heads off, leaving Melissa to watch the well-dressed masses enjoy her handiwork. In the distance, the carousel she ordered spins into the night, casting rays of light onto the ice. Melissa squints. Who is on the ice? She peers further, thinking she can make out someone crouched down. *That better not be someone playing a joke on me—or on anyone, for that matter.*

"Rumor has it that one year this guy ordered fifty thousand dollars worth of caviar and spread it on the ice." Melissa turns to hear James go on. "Turns out he didn't even like the stuff—just wanted to say he'd done it."

With Matron's words ringing in her ears; the guy she's liked so much standing in front of her; and an outfit that for once doesn't involve frills, puffy down coats, or a limp, Melissa feels decent. *In fact, I feel bold. Maybe it's the air, or the fact that this is it—this is the pinnacle of the week and it's a success all because of me. But I feel good.* She touches the twists Dove put in her hair and secured with tiny silver flowers. Her champagne-colored gown is cinched at the waist, and the silk shoulder wrap she has is lined with fleece to keep her warm even away from the heat lamps.

"Is that what I was?" Melissa asks James, her newfound boldness giving her the boost she needs to say what's on her mind. *What was I to him, anyway? Enough beating around the proverbial bush and out with it.*

James stands with one hand in his pocket, the other around his drink—some caramel-colored liquid set off by maraschino cherries. "What do you mean?"

"That guy you mentioned. The one who smeared caviar? He did what he did because he *could*. . . ." Melissa pauses, stepping so she's directly in front of James. "Not because he *liked* it. Or in this case, *her*."

James drains his drink, obviously caught off guard. "I don't why you're saying this, Mesilla."

"My name's Melissa, James. I think we've covered enough ground to at least go by that."

James nods. They stand in silence while Melissa tries again to see what's happening on the ice. General chaos and noises erupt from over in that direction. *If it's some posh kids I'll banish them from the ball. If it's a prince, then I guess he can slather caviar. . . .*

"I did like you, you know."

"Did?" Melissa hears the past tense and wonders why she doesn't feel worse. *Sure, it stings. Yes, there's a part of me that feels dejected. But then there's a larger part that isn't fazed by him. Is it possible to think you like someone more than you do? It's as though I got swept up in the idea of liking him, not the real him. Or maybe the Wonderland boosted me more than I thought.* "Is this about Charlie?"

"It's about competition," James says enigmatically.

"Meaning?" Melissa watches a lone figure come off the ice, and can see his tuxedo-clad self walking this way, carrying a tray of something. Is he a waiter gone astray?

"Meaning . . ." James takes Melissa by the shoulders, one hand on either side of her, and pulls her in the way he'd done during the blizzard.

She gives in to the kiss for a minute, wanting to want it, but feeling that somewhere inside of her is a voice saying *No, not this way. Not him.* If not him, then who? The answer comes to her right when she pulls away.

"Oh, sorry to bother you." The voice in the darkness, the one belonging to the waiter-slash-tuxedo, is Gabe's. Even in the dim light, Melissa can see his smile fade.

"You look great," Gabe says to her. He nods to James. "Well, I'm heading back to the chalet."

Melissa's cheeks burn with the kiss she didn't want, with the feelings she might have buried inside. "So soon? It's just getting started."

Gabe shakes his head. "Not for me, I think." James snakes his hand around Melissa's waist. She's so distracted by Gabe's impending departure that she doesn't bother shrugging him off.

"Wait, Gabe."

"No," Gabe says, his voice calm in the cold air. "I've done as much waiting as I'm going to do."

Melissa watches his silvery blond hair as he traces the path back to the chalet. James squeezes her waist, making her remember where she is and who she's left with. "What was that about?"

James smirks. "As I was saying . . . competition."

Melissa's face tells the story of being used. "So I'm the prize? Or wait—not even? You just tried to get me away from Gabe?"

James shrugs, his face looking like the nice guy Melissa thought he was, but his body language telling a different story. "You win some, you lose some. But me—I like winning."

Music swells as the band plays a lively tune, causing the gowns and dinner jackets to dance, twirling like a Victorian toy on the floor. Melissa calmly turns to James, who holds his hand out to dance with her. Leaving him hanging, she says, "Well, consider this a first. You just lost. Big time."

Melissa storms off, heading for the ice to make sure everything is as perfect as can be. On the way, Charlie flings her a couple of mean looks and Melissa lets them roll off her as she trudges onto the ice. *I won't slip. I won't slip.* She falls onto her butt, her legs in front of her. *Fine. So I slipped. Like anyone saw.*

A laugh lets her know someone did see her.

"Dove?"

"The one and only." Dove comes onto the ice, stepping like a pixie in her ballet flats. "Rough night?"

Melissa thinks about it. "You know what? No. It's fine. I'm . . . fine." She stands up and looks for evidence of caviar slathering or other pranks. Then, off by the edge under the shelter of a drooping pine tree, she sees something on the ice. "Come on, Dove."

They go toward it, looking. "Oh . . . oh . . ."

"Oh yeah," Dove says, and crouches to look.

Melissa puts her hands on the ice, seeing again her own reflection, but this time as a Botticelli, emerging from a shell with her hair cascading down. "It's beautiful. I'm . . ."

"You're beautiful," Dove says. "In the gown you have on or just in a red snowsuit. You are. You just don't believe it yet."

Melissa traces her own face on the ice, marveling at the likeness. "Who did this? It's got to be . . ."

"The same artist as the *Mona Lisa*."

Melissa shakes her head. "Who knows?" Her whole body pulsates with the knowledge that someone, whoever it is, did this for her.

"I know." Melissa looks up to see Gabe standing near

her with a tray of paints and squeeze bottles. Her surprise at seeing him is outmatched only by the sensation of each cell inside her zooming around, amazed, confused, incredulous at Gabe's gesture. *All along, this is how he felt?* Melissa wonders.

Dove opens her mouth. "I'll leave you two alone. I'm heading to the chair lift for a better view."

As Dove glides away, Melissa stands up, face-to-face with Gabe and his paints. "Why didn't you tell me?"

"I tried to before. But now . . ." Gabe looks away.

"It's not what you think," Melissa starts to say, thinking back to the kiss James planted on her.

"That's what people always say when it's exactly that." Gabe sits on the ice and begins blotting out the painting, spraying black ink onto the shell, then up so it begins to cover the flowing tresses.

"Don't—" Melissa grabs his arm. Gabe shrugs her off. Feeling totally dejected, and a bit shell-shocked, Melissa stands with her hands clenched. The two stay there in silence as Gabe finishes covering the picture, and then, when he's done, walks away.

At the base of the chair lift, Dove contemplates her options. *I could go back and pack right now, or try to get one last look at Max.* She stands in the halo of light, wondering what her next move will be, when she sees him coming toward her. *How Shakespearean,* she thinks, *to have a mixup in identities for Melissa, to have star-crossed lovers for me, and everything confused now.*

Decked out in a velvet jacket and black trousers, Max looks every inch the stylish gentleman. In her simple sheath dress and wrap, Dove thinks they could be the picture-perfect couple. Only, what would the caption say?

"So, you heading up for a run?" Max gestures to the chair lift. His voice is steady but his eyes dance as he looks at her.

"Thinking about it."

"You're doing a lot of thinking these days."

"Better than just grabbing people and kissing them," Dove answers.

"Look, that was pure coincidence." Max's face is awash with regret. His body leans toward her, reaching.

"Oh, I'm sure." Dove leans away from him, trying to be immune.

Max looks smug. "You think I planted Claire there? Why would I do that when you know you're . . ."

"Leaving?" Dove interrupts. "You asked me at the beginning of the week to choose whether you should stay or go."

"The infamous Clash song question." Max shifts from one foot to the other.

Dove watches him move around, wondering if he's

cold or nervous or both. "Yeah, only it turns out I'm the one who should go." Dove takes a long hard look at her tall would-be suitor. "So I am."

Max's face remains calm and even, but his hands shake. "So that's it?" Max finally gives way to his emotions, reaching for her shoulders with both hands. "Don't. Don't go . . . just . . . I never liked her. All this time it was—"

Dove shakes her head. "Then why'd you do it? You have one hell of a way of showing devotion. . . ."

Max grips her firmly, unable to let go. "How is it that I'm meant to be devoted and you get to plan a trip into someone else's arms?"

Dove looks at him, a flash of their embraces, talks, potential academic futures coming to her in a wash of images and feelings. "It's too late, Max." Her chest feels weighted but she keeps with her intent. "I leave first thing in the morning for Nevis."

"Well." Max coughs to cover up his quaking voice. His eyes still hold her but his hands drop, defeated. "Be sure to give my best to my family if you bump into them at the top-notch hotels and restaurants."

"I doubt I'll be frequenting those." Dove suddenly wonders where, exactly, she will be going, what she'll be doing aside from reuniting with William.

"I guess you have to do what you have to do." Max steps forward into the halo of light. *He could kiss me, he's so close. But he wouldn't. But what if he did? Would it change things? Prove something?* He doesn't. He puts his palm on Dove's alabaster cheek for a minute and, ever the gentleman, says, "Take care."

Melissa tells everything to Dove, and she reciprocates, as they watch the chair lift swing by. "Sorry about Max."

Dove picks at her cuticles. "Don't be. I'm making my own decisions, which is what I wanted to do. You can't have it all, right? If there were two of me and one could go one way and the other could follow a different path . . ." Her sentence evaporates as she slides Chapstick onto her lips and looks at the star-studded night sky. "And what about you, Mel?"

"Oh, who knows? Do you think Charlie's really with James? Do I even care? Seems I have a knack for picking the wrong guy." Melissa touches her lips, feeling the place on the side where James kissed her.

"Really? Seems to me like you picked the right one all along." Dove tugs at her wispy hair.

"Meaning?"

"Meaning—you told me how you liked Gabe all last year, and then you liked him when you first got to Les Trois. *James* was the distraction. Not Gabe. He's been your friend, the one who picked you up when you fell, the one to invite you here, the one . . ."

"The one for me." Melissa smiles, wiping away tears. *If only I hadn't shoved the thing with James in his face . . .*

Back by the ice, Melissa is dismayed to see her portrait almost entirely covered over, dark as the rest of the ice. She looks closely. *The only thing left is my eyes.*

"I couldn't cover them." Gabe emerges from the wooded edge of the pond and stands with paint-stained hands, looking at his handiwork.

"How come?"

"Did you ever meet someone who just . . ." He stops.

"Got you? Or came to your rescue when you fell? Or thought you looked great in a stupid red snowsuit? Or who wished she'd been with you the whole time instead of fawning over some competitive friend?" Melissa slides the words out of her mouth, not once feeling embarrassed.

"You do realize that out of this whole silly resort, this whole country, this whole globe, you're the only person I've ever painted?" He pauses, taking a few steps closer to her. "Actually, if truth be told, you're the first person in years that I thought was *worth* painting. I pretty much got used to doing landscapes or abstracts."

Gabe stands inches away from her. Melissa reaches for one of his streaked hands and interlaces their fingers.

"Why me? And when did you learn to paint?"

"One question at a time. First, because you're the one who inspired me. Who invaded my thoughts so that you were the art I was looking at." He shakes his head. "Sorry if that sounds lame. And second, I had a ski accident when I was fourteen. Rehabbed at the same place as this big-time artist. Learned a thing or two."

"Aren't you just Mister Industrious?"

"Is that how you see me?" Gabe moves closer.

"Not really. Why? How do you want me to see you?"

"Like this." Gabe puts his hands on Melissa's head, bringing her to him, kissing her deeply. The cold air settles around them, and as they kiss it's all they can do not to fall over on the ice. The more intense the kissing, the more Melissa forgets about James, about anything other than just Gabe, until they begin to sway, and then, suddenly, reeling, wind up knocked onto the ice. Melissa winces briefly, then feels her rib pain ease up.

Laughing, Gabe looks at Melissa. He spreads her hair out around her head. "Now you really look like a Botticelli."

"And you look like . . ."

"A smitten artist?" Gabe leans down and kisses her again.

"I should sit up," Melissa says. "If Matron finds me like this she'll banish me from the ball."

Gabe kisses her again and makes a face. "Nah, she wouldn't dare. I'd tell her it's my last night's wish."

Melissa's smile fades. "What do you mean?" She sits up, feeling the ice seep through her dress.

Gabe looks concerned. "You didn't know? I thought James—I thought he'd have mentioned . . ."

"No."

"The ski team. We're leaving. Austria for practice, then Denmark and Norway for competing."

The words hang heavy as wet snow in the air as the band's music stops. Over the microphone, Charlie's voice comes into the air. "I'd like to thank the band for allowing me to talk. I have an announcement." Melissa stands up, not knowing whether to focus on Gabe's bad news or Charlie's.

"I wasn't trying to deceive you, Melissa," Gabe says.

"Ladies and gentlemen. Thanks to the wonderful paparazzi here who so kindly took photos of me with . . . my boyfriend James Marks-Benton . . . I have been selected to be the next face of Young American Cosmetics! I leave for Los Angeles next week."

Melissa barely hears the rest. "Looks like everyone's taking off." Her sadness is palpable. Gabe looks at her, clearly wishing he could take away the pain of the moment, but he can't. He touches her hand lightly. "If it's meant to be it's meant to be, right?" she asks, fighting tears.

He nods, his silvery hair illuminated in the night air. "Right."

"Maybe you'll come back?"

Gabe nods. "Nothing's set in stone, okay?"

Melissa nods, swallowing her sadness and tears, and is determined to look strong even if she feels rejected and empty. *He won't be back. Not until the season's over, at least, and by then he'll meet someone else or forget me, or I'll forget how it feels to be with him.*

Finding every bit of courage she has, Melissa kisses Gabe, hugs him, and then adds, "Just keep in touch, okay? Maybe our paths will cross someday."

"One can only hope." Gabe grabs for her. "Don't go."

Melissa walks off, feeling new tears welling up that she can't fend off. "I'm not the one who is."

Wordlessly, Dove and Melissa ride the empty chair lift.

At the top of the mountain, Melissa and Dove look at the twinkling lights below and step onto the frozen ground.

"You can hear the music all the way up here."

"You sound sad." Dove wrinkles her mouth at Melissa.

"Well, you're leaving. Of course I'm sad. Who will I talk to? Who'll make me fresh rolls and sort out my dramas?" Melissa sighs, thinking about Gabe and James. "Not that I'm likely to have any dramas with the ski boys vacating. You realize you're leaving me here to wither with Charlie. . . ."

"Well, when you say it like that, I have no choice." Dove pokes Melissa in the shoulder so she'll look at her instead of the party below.

"No choice but to feel guilty?"

"No. No choice but to ask you to come with me." Dove's eyes shine with excitement. "Before you say forget it, just think: you, me, the beach. Or the other way—you, Charlie, the cold."

"But I don't . . ."

"Have a ticket? We'll get you one at the airport."

Melissa's heart thumps so loud she feels as though she's competing with the music's bass line below. "But I don't have . . ."

"Clothes? We'll get some there. And money? You've made great tips, right?"

Melissa clenches her fists, thinking. "Presumably Harley's been working down there, so maybe she'd have a job or two she could hook us up with. . . ."

"Now you're thinking." Dove cracks a big smile, crouches down into the snow, and comes up bearing a big snowball. "Just think, this time tomorrow we could be making sand castles instead."

"And Max?" Melissa asks.

"Well, Claire's booked until nearly the end of the month. He can stay here and ski with her all he likes. Term at Oxford doesn't start until the end of January . . ." She pauses, realizing that if she wanted to try to go back to school, there might just be enough time for her to enroll. "And if Shakespeare and English texts call to me louder than the waves, then maybe I'll look into it. But for now—despite the fact that he's been incommunicado—I'm heading to William." A brief look of concern washes over Dove's face, but then she pulls herself together, thinking of seeing him at the airport.

"And I'm . . . ?" Melissa looks out at the expansive resort, the lost kisses, the dreams of romance, the hours of work put into cooking, hosting, and making the wonderland a reality. "If I'm so good at putting together this major event, then I think I can allow myself a detour."

"A sidetrack?" Dove brings her knees to her chest, excited by the potential of what's to come, the warmth that will soon cover her.

"A fork in the road," Melissa says. "We have to pack, leave a note for Matron, say our good-byes, and go. Hey—wouldn't it be fun to meet up with Harley again? Assuming she hasn't been kicked off the island?"

"So you're coming?" Dove grabs her hands and they race toward the chairlifts. "This is amazing!" She pauses. "And yeah, who knows what Harley's been up to."

"This is incredible," Melissa agrees. "A drinkless toast—to moving onward and upward."

"To a New Year."

"To us, on a plane in eight hours, heading to paradise."

They raise their imaginary glasses and get ready to head . . .

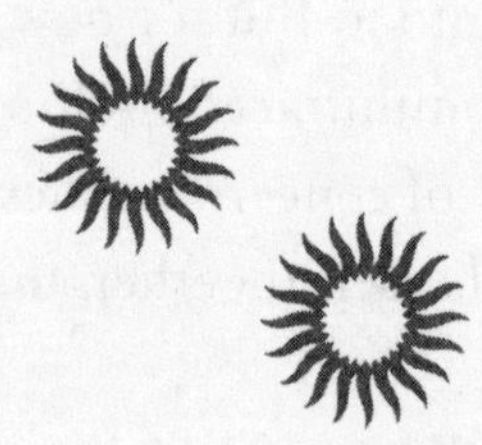

Off the Trails

Chalet Girls, Book 3

Coming in February 2008

Follow the Chalet Girls to the tropical islands,
where the surf is cool, the sand is smooth,
and the boys are hot.

Turn the page for a sneak peek at

Off the Trails

by

Emily Franklin

Look for it in February 2008.

Scanning the faces for whichever boy could be the infamous William, Melissa nearly crashes into the person in front of her.

"Watch it!" Tanned to perfection though she's only just arriving, and dressed in Indian-print fabric that's wound into a halter-style dress, the girl huffs as she removes a bit of trailing fabric from under Melissa's shoe. "Ever heard of walking properly?"

Melissa's gut instinct is to come back with some sarcastic comment, but she's too busy wondering which boy beauty is William, and how Dove will react when she's finally in his arms. *Hell, if I can't find love myself, I may as well live vicariously through others.*

When she realizes the girl is waiting for her to bow or fawn all over her for the minor tactical error in coordination, Melissa volunteers this: "Oh, madam, I'm so terribly sorry to have inconvenienced you." Inside, she sticks her tongue out, but her exterior remains fixed.

"Are you just going to stand there and not apologize?" Impatient for a reply, the bronzed and annoyed girl pouts her perfectly glossed lips, lifts her oversized pouchy blue leather bag onto her shoulder, and rolls her eyes. "Guess you don't have much to offer in the way of decency or class."

Determined to at least respond, Melissa feels her mouth fly open, but the girl beats her to the punch and walks away. Watching her walk into the throngs of people collecting at the baggage and arrival areas, Melissa hopes this particular girl isn't a fair representation of the other people she'll meet on the island. The girl's blue leather bag bounces as she walks away, leaving Melissa with a bad taste in her mouth.

Melissa rummages through her pockets, flustered from the interaction, and searches for gum.

"Hey, what's wrong?" Dove, breathless from hauling her bags on the sandy linoleum floor, stands before Melissa expectantly.

"Nothing—just a brief encounter with one of those mythical characters, the Beach Bitch. You know the type: all glamour, no reality. Giant bag to hold all her evils." Melissa rolls her eyes, eager to forget the run-in. "But enough about that—what about you? Where is he? I can't wait to meet William!"

"*You* can't wait?" Dove grins. "What about me?" She begins to search the crowd for William's face—the same face that caught her eye so many months back, the same one that has appeared in her dreams over the time they'd been apart, making her sure that flying here was the right thing to do. "I'll find him—you find your bags. That way we can just go right away to William's house."

Melissa nods. "Sure. Sounds good." She heads off to watch luggage circle round and round on the conveyor belt, hoping to see her red duffel bag. *Black, green, plaid, floral, ugly yellow*—she says the colors in her head as the various suitcases spin past. *Don't even tell me they lost it.* All around her, fellow passengers claim their luggage and head off to start their vacations. *But what about me?* Melissa doesn't give in to the small panic. Instead she waits for her bag.

After all the luggage has emptied and her bag is nowhere to be found, Melissa plunges into the dwindling crowd of people to find Dove.

"Take me away from this place," Melissa orders, swinging her arms around to indicate the small airport. "I'm ready to collapse on the beach. Even if I have no clothing, no bathing suit, and no flip-flops to my name."

The small features on Dove's face look sullen. "I can't find him."

Here I am worrying about my bag, and she can't find her boy. "Okay . . . maybe he's late?"

"Maybe." Dove eyes the faces again, hoping for a glimpse of the sign with her name on it, or just of William, barefooted and tan, smiling at her newly cropped hair. Instinctually she touches the ends of her pixie cut, fanning the silvery bangs over her forehead. "Maybe he's late. Or maybe . . ." She hates to say it, but does. "Or maybe he just forgot."

"Oh, Dove." Melissa gives one more glance over her shoulder at the luggage rack, but doesn't see her red duffel. Normally she'd wait and wait and then approach the baggage-claim help center, but right now she knows what Dove needs. "You know what? Let's just take off." She raises her dark eyebrows. "We'll grab a cab, head to the nearest beach, and kick back with something fruity as we watch the waves." Dove doesn't look so sure. "After all, it is New Year's Day, and people are sleeping off their revelry, right? So we'll relax, too."

"And reality?" Dove's voice and face don't seem entirely convinced.

"Meaning?" Melissa asks, edging Dove and her stuff out the sliding glass doors to the taxi stand.

"What about William? And what about meeting up

again with Harley, our old bunkmate? And what about money or a job or place to stay?"

"All very good points." Melissa nods as though she's in a business meeting. "But ones that will have to wait until we have sand in our toes and sun on our cheeks." Dove crosses her arms, doubtful. Melissa does her best to reassure. "Am I or am I not the queen of planning and pressure? Did I or did I not single-handedly pull off a fancy ball for hundreds of people while nursing broken ribs and a very bruised ego?"

Dove gives in. As they step into the heat of the afternoon, the warm air envelops them, sending their shoulders down. Dove peels off her long-sleeved shirt and adjusts her tank top straps. "It does feel good to be something other than cold."

"Oh, you're something other than cold, alright," says a voice from behind her.

Dove knows this voice. It could only belong to one person. The one guy she absolutely doesn't want to see right now after having been stood up by William.

Melissa chimes in, "Oh, you mean hot—something other than cool. I get it."

Dove blushes and swats a hand at Melissa's side. She turns so that she is in full view of him. Him. "Max. What the hell are you doing here?" Dove looks at his rumpled shirt, his similarly disheveled khakis, his too-pale feet sticking out of his flip-flops.

Max, immune to Dove's seeming lack of pleasure at seeing him, pats her on the back. "You didn't think I'd miss a family holiday, did you?"

Dove's face remains stony. Of course. His parents are here. His siblings are here. Here, being taken care of by Harley, the supposed hostess. "I guess I thought you'd stay snowbound. Or at the very least go back to Oxford."

"Oh, you know school doesn't start for ages," Max explains, pushing a hand through his cocoa-colored hair. "Plenty of time for a break at the Sugar Hut."

"The what?" Melissa interjects.

"The Sugar Hut," Max says, hailing a cab. "Family accommodations." He slings his bags into the trunk and opens the door to climb in, staring at Dove. "Speaking of accommodations, where are you two headed?"

Melissa opens her mouth to say they have no idea, but Dove grabs her wrist and covers up. "Don't you worry about that, Max. You just take care of yourself."

Max slides into the cab, and sticks his head out the window. "Well," he sighs, searching Dove's face for any signs of like, love, or even lust, "if you need anything, just come to the hut."

The taxi peels away, leaving Dove and Melissa in a small cloud of sand and grit.

"The Sugar Hut," Melissa says, committing the name to memory. "Always good to have a fallback plan."

"I can't believe he's here," Dove says. Inside, her pulse races from being too close to Max again, too close to her years of liking him, too close to how she'd nearly fallen for him instead of coming here for William. *Maybe I picked the wrong guy,* Dove thinks, looking one last time for William.

"Should we go?" Melissa flags down a cab. The heat prickles up her arm and she wishes she had something—anything—to change into. "I'm going to need a trip into town. Anywhere I can grab a few items to wear."

Dove nods. "Right. Of course." *My boy troubles can wait for a while.* Gathering up her strength and pocketing her disappointment over William's lame showing and Max's intensity, Dove puts on a brave face. "I say we head right over to the Pulse, this tiny little boutique that has—"

"Sounds expensive," Melissa says, money worries creeping back in.

Remembering her own financial woes, Dove bites her top lip in the center. It wouldn't be fun to browse and pine for things she can never have, but it might be nice to at least see what's out there. *Maybe Melissa's right, and we should just figure out where to go, where to sleep, and how to find William.* Momentarily Dove ponders his whereabouts: On the beach? Working? Rubbing lotion onto another girl's bare back? Her stomach turns just picturing it.

"I'd love a shopping spree—even a mini one, trust

me," Melissa says, slipping her pile of dark hair back into a simple elastic.

"Well, this island isn't really the place for a massive shopping binge, but you can stumble onto some cool finds."

"Sounds fun, but . . ." The heat pads the air, making beads of sweat appear on her upper lip. She wipes them away and adds, "But it's not worth blowing all of the tips I made at Les Trois. I mean, think back to all that hard work. You don't want to waste it on a sarong or something, do you?"

"No, I guess not." Dove's excitement begins to flag. What, after all, does she have going for her? No long-term boyfriend waiting for her with a rose or other clichéd token of his affections, no swanky hotel to go to, no promising party or plan for the night or days to follow, and not enough money to fund any of the above. "Where is my fairy godmother? If only there was a way to buy stuff without having to pay . . ."

"Well, there isn't," Melissa says. "Let's get practical and hop on a tram." The pastel-colored trams have a certain appeal to Melissa—the open windows, the jostling crowd headed into town, being on the move rather than stuck at the airport. "Besides, it's bound to be cheaper than a taxi." She wipes her forehead. "I'm going to need a cold drink before I start pounding the pavement for a new job. No shopping for us just yet . . ."

As soon as the words are out, settling into the tropical air, Dove grins. "Not true . . ."

Melissa looks skeptical. "How do you figure?" She pats her pocket to remind her friend of its emptiness.

Dove raises her eyebrows, looking like an excited doll. "What if . . . we charged it?" She pauses, thinking. "To my parents, who I believe still have several accounts around the island. One of which is bound to be at the Pulse . . ."

Melissa opens her mouth in surprise. "Dove, you wouldn't dare! I mean, didn't they specifically tell you that you're cut off from—"

Newly confident in her decision, Dove flags a taxi. She opens the door, chucks her bags into the open trunk, and climbs in. She pats the seat next to her so that Melissa will join her, and smiles. "True. *They* cut me off financially. But then again, *they* aren't *here*. They're stuck back in the frigid countryside of England. I haven't asked them for a penny since the summer. Nearly six months of self-sufficiency. They won't find out for ages, by which point I'll be able to pay them back with the loads of cash I make at the new fabulous job I've yet to find." Melissa hesitates before climbing in next to Dove, wishing her luggage had made the trip to Nevis with her, wishing she hadn't left Gabe behind—or been left—and wishing wholeheartedly that she had a job to give her some security.

"Maybe one T-shirt or something, but that's it," Melissa says as the taxi pulls away from the curb. "But I'll pay for it. It just wouldn't be right to scribble down your parents' names on a charge slip."

Dove slicks some gloss over her lips and looks out the window, her heart pulsing rapidly. "You'd be surprised at just how easy it is. . . ." She turns to Melissa and squeezes her hand. "Besides, what's a holiday without a few surprises?"

About the Author

Emily Franklin is the author of the *Chalet Girls* books and the *Principles of Love* series, as well as the novel *The Other Half of Me*. Her two novels for adults are *The Girls' Almanac* and *Liner Notes*. She has edited several anthologies, including *It's a Wonderful Lie: 26 Truths about Life in Your Twenties*. She lives in Massachusetts with her family.